THE WAKE-UP CALL

Jonas Eriksson

ACKNOWLEDGEMENTS

First of all, big thanks to designer Etienne Bugeja for crafting the fantastic cover – it has played a key role in the success of the book. I also want to thank my group of first-time readers and friends for reading the book and giving me great input. And I want to extend extra gratitude to my mother for always believing in me and my endeavors, to Aiden for reminding me that the world is a fun and not so damn serious place, and to Lenah for being my muse, my best critic, my editor and my love.

THE WAKE-UP CALL

Can you believe it? Because I sure can't. I'm on a blind date with Gwen Parks. It's really more like a "mute date" than a blind date, at least for me, because it would be hard to find a more boring person than Gwen – even if I looked at the Senior Citizen's Stamp Collection Association. She's close to giving me a brain hemorrhage and we've been sitting at an over-pretentious French restaurant in midtown Manhattan for 32 minutes.

Yes, I've counted them.

It's not like she isn't talking, no, quite the opposite. The problem is, she's not saying anything. I'm not sure if it's because she's nervous or just ignorant, but she just goes on and on, without a single thought towards whether I'm interested in what she's saying or not. She's also on a namedropping mission, talking about people I don't know, have never heard about, have no interest in ever knowing, and she's talking about them like they were mutual friends of ours. All I'm doing is saying "yes", "aha", and "oh" in approximately the right places while trying hard not to fall asleep.

I'm also trying to get drunk, having a more interesting date with this 200-dollar bottle of Gevrey-Chambertin we're drinking. "We" have nearly finished the bottle and I can't remember Gwen making a refill. But how could she, as she's talking all the time? When the food gets here I hope she stops her blabbering for a bit, at least while chewing. I'm starving both for food and more interesting company.

She's looking good though, a classy broad, this Gwen. She's eloquent, posh and dresses elegantly. Her short crème dress is flattering her slightly stocky, but nice legs and she has a gingerbread man tan, probably from a spray tanning salon. The only turnoff - except for her constant talking - is her mouth, which is covered in red lipstick. This makes her and most other women look like clowns. I know people have strange turn-ons these days, but making out with Bozo was never one of mine.

I blame my best friend Mike Kowalski for setting me up on this so called date with his bodacious blonde colleague. He says it's about time I find myself a good, reliable and intelligent woman, which makes him sound like my mother, or at least what my mother would've sounded like if she were like most mothers (and alive). Apparently he thinks Gwen possesses these qualities, although he ought to know that finding a permanent partner is a lot more complex than presenting two lists of suitable personality specs and matching them. I know this from experience, having had many relations, but few relationships - something which irks Mike, but then again, I guess he's just jealous about my good looks.

Mike's absolutely right though that my record with women is based more on quantity than quality, at least when you look at the intelligence and maturity level of some of the girls I've "dated", but I guess I'm not alone in falling for the wrong kind. Good thing I realize my mistakes and end them before they get too complicated, right? I wish Mike himself would've had the balls to do that, because then he wouldn't have stayed with plain-looking and open-legged Joanne (who I usually refer to as Ho-Anne).

There are many reasons I don't like Joanne, but to keep it short, it would suffice to say she's a bitch. This was clear to me from the first time I met her. I remember it like yesterday. Mike and I were at lunch when he announced he would be bringing someone to my party. I was shocked at first, because I hadn't heard anything about this date and he'd been single so long I wondered if he'd ever get back on the horse again. Average-looking people like Mike are usually not very happy on their own, because they don't get the confidence boost from frequently hooking up with new women, something I've done excessively thanks to my nice apartment, my platinum VISA card and inheriting my father's good features.

Anyway, when Mike announced he'd met someone, I couldn't help but think desperation must have struck him badly. But I of course hoped he'd bring a nice, friendly and down-to-earth girl.

Enter Joanne, who looked uncomfortable from the second she put her foot in my penthouse. She clung to Mike the whole evening like he was her lifeboat in a sea of unknown evil, but she didn't stick to him in a cute, we-are-freshly-in-love kind of way, but more like she wanted to make sure he didn't pay attention to anyone else but her. She whispered in his ear, tugged at him like a spoiled child, and hardly said a word to me.

They left early of course.

This was an omen for things to come. I guess I could have understood what Mike saw in her if she was very attractive – but Joanne isn't. She looks ten years older than her age (which I think is 32), her skin is as lifeless as a lifelong smokers' and her voice is coarser than a witch's croak. She always wears short skirts and tight tops, but the only curve on her body is her crooked ego.

As if this isn't enough in the minus column, I strongly suspect she's cheating. Not at Scrabble, but on my best friend. I'm 99 percent sure about this after hearing from Mike about flirtatious text message exchanges with other guys (she claims they're just friends) and lots of nights "out" ending with her coming home in the wee hours of the morning - two things that spell disaster for any relationship. And her appetite for the nightlife makes him worry to death about her, which he doesn't deserve, as I've told him countless times.

And what does Mike do? He defends her of course! He's so brainwashed by her controlling claws he doesn't see what kind of she-monster she really is. He's miserable and deep down I think he knows it. But why would he take my relationship advice? To him, I'm "Jack the dipper", a nickname which might've been flattering if I was still in college, but I'm not. I'm 35.

"How about you, Jack?" says Gwen and wakes me up from my thinking about Mike and his love troubles. I have no idea what she's talking about, as I haven't really been listening.

"About me?" I echo.

"Yes, are you investing in anything?"

Okay, the stock market again. The stock market and her fantastic father - two of Gwen's favorite things to talk about and coincidentally two of the most mind-numbing topics of all time. I don't really give a fuck about her father or the stock market. It's very un-American of me, but money bores me - probably because I have lots of it.

"Not really, I put them in the bank and fuhgeddabout them."

"Well, I thought since Mike's really into these things you'd be too. Anyway, my father thinks the market will…"

I fade out again. I look at her lips moving. They're nice and full and would look so much better if they could remain closed. I drift to work. How's the soup campaign going? How do you make soup sexy? Soup is soup. Maybe that's a slogan? Did I reply to Nicholas e-mail? I could sneak out my trusted Blackberry, but I'm not drunk enough yet to be that rude. I need to remember that this is Mike's colleague and try my best to control myself. But of course I wouldn't mind sleeping with her and there's a good chance of that if I just play my cards remotely right. There usually is.

My mind is an over-active hub. It's always on and the only way I can shut it off is by drinking a generous amount of alcohol. You could say I drink to numb the pain, the pain from not being in the place I want to be - at work and in life in general. It used to be pleasant to think about the agency, especially a few years back, when things were looking brighter than a sunburned blonde's bleached smile and I was on the cover of business magazines as one of the shining stars in the advertising world. Now I'm more like the captain on a sinking ship, running back and forth among the rats on deck, while trying to dodge enemy cannonballs. Okay, it's maybe not that bad yet, but if we lose another big account I'm going to have a friggin' heart attack.

I ought to book a meeting with my business partner and agency co-owner Nicholas Green, but he's always busy with his other business commitments, start-ups and partnerships. But I need that meeting so I better call him. When would be a good time? Whoa, my brain is in my Outlook, need to dig it out, need to focus on what Gwen's saying. Naaw, that's no good, I look at her breasts instead. They're nice and full and I wonder if they're her own. Yeah, they must be, they wouldn't be sitting up like that without a push-up bra, which I'm thankful for because it gives me an ample view of cleavage. I love cleavage. But there's bad cleavage and good cleavage. Too much of a gap and it's bad cleavage. How do you keep eye contact when a woman has cleavage like that? My eyes wander: eyes, breasts, eyes, breasts. Can she tell? Does she mind? She has a cute smile, but her face is maybe a little wide and round, which reminds me of some animal. Not really a chipmunk, but more like a teenage mutant ninja turtle, if that counts for an animal. Donatello, Rafael? Who were those other ninja turtles? Splinter? No, that was the rat.

As a saving grace from my whirring brain, here comes the food, but sadly in small, artistically challenged portions. I agree food should look good, but it doesn't mean you have to create art with it. I get so tired of these fancy, overpriced places sometimes, but you can't impress a girl with a Big Mac and a milkshake, believe me I've tried. Tonight I just wanted a plate of pasta, two bottles of red wine and a decent chance of getting laid, not this hollow conversational torture and *cuisine le microscopice*. But Gwen is apparently in love with everything French - the food, the people, the language and the wine, and that's why she's enjoying this place, where the waiters have thick accents, hairy arms and their large bony noses high in the air like they just suffered a severe case of cocaine nosebleed. It feels like we're in Paris and I don't like Paris. I've been there twice and never got across the cultural divide and the rudeness. Gwen even placed the order in French - something which got the waiter all sparkly-eyed and likely even more in love with himself and his country.

I order another bottle of red to dampen my growing irritation.

"Amazing right?" Gwen says, piercing me with her green eyes. "Don't you just love the way they serve the food here? Each plate is a treat for the senses."

She takes a bite of her white fish, chews it slowly, utters a lengthy "mmm" and looks at me big-eyed, like she's waiting for me to agree.

"That was just what I was thinking, Gwen." I lie, "Excellent choice." And I raise my glass towards her and as we toast, I lock my eyes with hers. I give her the Jack-wants-you-look, which has lured women into my arms since 1984 or something like that. I should have a sign or some kind of stamp made, signaling I'm tested and quality assured. (But sadly my love also comes with an expiration date.)

We clink our glasses and the way she looks at me I'm pretty sure I'm in the clear when it comes to post-dinner *sexercise*. I just need to stay on the right side of shitfaced.

I take a bite of food and I'm immediately disappointed by my rib-eye - ordered medium-rare, but definitely more towards medium. But I wolf it down anyway, as I'm now so hungry Ronald McDonald's left rubber foot would've been a treat.

I eat rapidly in an effort to focus on anything else than Gwen's squeaky voice and I wash everything down with my fifth or possibly sixth (who's counting anyway?) glass of red. I smile at Gwen. I smile at her because she's not talking right now and it makes me happy. Although while she's eating, I've noticed she has a very annoying habit of cleaning her teeth with her tongue. It's quite un-lady-like and doesn't suit her otherwise faultless style.

Gwen is also a slow eater and I think she spends more time investigating her food (besides talking of course) than actually putting it in her mouth. It's another annoying thing I have to bear with, if only for the chance of nighttime release. I have a lot of stress built up and sex is my favorite way of getting it out of me.

Tonight I'm even more tense than usual and with every glass of wine I'm getting more and more annoyed with Gwen, her constant talking and her uptight ways. I know I really shouldn't be drinking this much, but once the train has left the station, I find it hard to put the brakes on. Besides, I see no other way to escape the deadly grasp of Gwen's *boredomia conversationalis*.

I take another healthy sip of wine, finish the glass, re-fill and feel waves of exhaustion crash on my internal shore. I'm not in the mood for dinner anymore, not in the mood for wasting my time nodding to Gwen and her stories about her idiot friends and their pointless careers. I need to do something dramatic.

Gwen's describing her soufflé like it has just given her an orgasm when the thought occurs to me that Gwen is a 60-year-old woman stuck in a 29-year-old body. I laugh out loud. I'm dating "grannies" now - Mike ought to be proud.

"What's so funny?" Gwen asks, giving me a puzzled look.

I compose myself, down my warm glass of Hennessy XO and look her straight in the eyes.

"You know, Gwen, I've got to be honest with you. I'm bored out of my pants. I can't stay in this shithole any longer. So we have two options: I pay the bill and we go to my place and fuck like bunnies or I pay the bill and go home to watch a movie. Either way, I leave now."

Gwen's eyes expand and her mouth drops.

"What?" she says. "Are you serious?"

"Yup," I say, and look around for the nearest waiter.

***

Mike might have set me up on the date, but it's not Mike who wakes me on Sunday morning - it's Stephen, the father. Yes, Stephen is the only one of my friends who has a child, which might sound a bit strange considering my age, but it's kind of typical for New York - a place where dreams come true - not kids. Meaning my dreams don't have any kids in them.

Stephen has been dreaming about kids though, ever since I got to know him back in university. He's in a rock solid relationship and has been for many years, but along with the birth of his son, Jeffrey, that ship might slowly be sinking. At least according to Stephen.

The problem is that baby Jeffrey doesn't like his father, in fact it appears he doesn't have any connection to him at all. He cries every time Stephen tries to carry him, play with him or any other fatherly activity and it's breaking poor Stephen's fragile heart. This strange emotional rift has created a lot of tension between Stephen and his wife Maria, and despite many counseling sessions, the key to their happiness seems to lay in Jeffrey's minuscule hands. It's an odd and sad situation and Stephen has been calling me at uncomfortable hours to talk about it. For some reason he thinks I know what to do, a guy who never had a relationship lasting longer than year, and who doesn't even like kids. I do my best and try to be a good friend and listener, although it's pretty difficult at times. I don't cope well with crying men, especially not those with a faint British accent.

"Hello," I mumble from my bed into my Blackberry. The sound of my own sleep-broken voice sends whips of pain to the back of my head. This is not the best way to start the day.

"Hi Jack, sorry for calling you this early. I hope I'm not disturbing you, but I really need to talk."

It's about now I realize Gwen Parks is lying next to me, snoring like a bus driver. I almost swallow my tongue.

"Sure, I'll call you back in twenty minutes, okay?" I whisper, then I hang up and look at Gwen.

I've woken up next to girls before of course - girls I like, girls I don't like and girls I didn't even know were there. I'm trained in these situations, I know how not to panic.

I rise slowly from bed so as not to wake her up. You should never wake a sleeping one-night stand - be quiet as a ninja.

But it's hard to be a ninja when it feels like you're walking out from a car accident. My legs wobble out into the kitchen, where the sun instantly hits me in the eye. It looks like a fine day in the Apple, but I think I just had a bite of worm.

On the marble kitchen table stands evidence of last night's decadence, a half-empty bottle of 30-year-old, ridiculously expensive and tarp-tasting Scottish malt whisky I got for my 35th birthday since I guess they couldn't find a bottle as old as I am. It's called Glen-something and it's rich enough for you to coat your boat with it. How I managed to empty half the bottle boggles my mind and hurts it too.

I silently open the fridge, take two Evian water bottles and head over to my renaissance-inspired Italian bathroom. I need to shower off the hangover, along with some of Gwen's body fluids. Yuck. I pray I had the decency to wear a condom.

But condom or no condom, I need to focus on feeling human again and get the hell out of here before Gwen wakes up and thinks we should start a relationship.

Or talk.

After rinsing her smell from my body, I write a note to the snoring "granny". My handwriting is shaky and resembles that of a five-year-old, but it's got nothing to do with the hangover, just my handwriting.

"Had to go to work. Help yourself to what you want. Best, Jack."

My lies are usually better than this.

***

It doesn't matter how hung-over you are or who you slept with the night before, Central Park is always a place of beauty (except for the odd hobo and midnight robber). This is where my mind winds down after a rough night and when I bought my Upper East Side penthouse a couple of years ago, it was on the top of my list - to be close to the park.

I grip the thermos coffee cup in my hand like it was a sacred object and take in the green, as much as I can under my hangover helmet. It's a bit sad to ruin this rather serene moment with a phone call to someone as depressed as Stephen, but a promise is a promise and a friend is a friend. I'm just about understanding this and it's about time, because I don't have many close friends left, and the ones I have are basically in meaningful or meaningless relationships - meaning they don't have much time to hang out with me. Not that I have much time to hang out with them either, being a workaholic and all.

I take a deep breath and sit down on a wooden bench. I scan the surroundings, but my vision is lagging slightly and everything around me seems to happen in slow motion. It's Sunday morning so there are basically only two types of people about - tourists and joggers. Not far from where I'm sitting, two squirrels are arguing about an acorn. I like squirrels, they remind me of Christmas. I watch a male jogger run by, his legs so hairy they seem tattooed. He's old but fit, clinging on to the years by his fingernails or by the hours spent in the gym. A young blonde woman power-walks past me the other way, looking pretty in her pink track top and her iPod strapped to her midsection like a life vest. It's the rush hour of jogging and although this is not Los Angeles, people sure want to look good. Good for them and good for me - gives me something to look at. I kind of envy these people who start the day feeling fresh and healthy, but I can't for the life of me go out for a jog. I was never a big eater and the extra pounds stay off anyway, so I might as well do something more fulfilling with my time. Like work. Or drinking. Or sex.

I take a sip from my piping hot Americano and dial Stephen's number. Am I ready for a crying man? We'll see.

Stephen picks up and says: "Hi Jack, how are you?" like he didn't just call me in desperation. This is the problem with being too polite, you end up wasting people's time asking things you don't really want to know nor care about. Being in advertising for almost all my working life has taught me that there are times for sugarcoating and times where you go straight to the point. You have to be able to choose your strategy based on the situation. With friends I don't waste time on the how are you-bullshit if I got something important to say. If they're real friends you don't need it. But since he asks, I'm going to tell him.

"I've got a hangover from hell and I just slept with an elderly lady trapped in a young woman's body. I've been better. I guess you didn't call me to ask me how I was?"

An insecure chuckle follows. Stephen is one of these guys who doesn't know how to react when somebody says something unexpected or crosses a social boundary - it's a typical defense mechanism of his. Then he gets to the point.

"I'm losing it, Jack, I'm on the verge of losing everything. Jeffrey still hates my guts and nobody understands why. Maria is distancing herself by the minute, she's probably already preparing the divorce papers. Her parents think there's something wrong with me. Maybe there is. Maybe I wasn't supposed to be a father." Stephen is already on the verge of tears and pushing out the words in haste, like he's about to break down any second. I understand him though, it's got to be tough wanting something so badly and for so long and then getting there only to find out it's not what you thought it would be. I can sympathize, having worked my ass off my whole life to reach my peak at 33. It's all downhill from here, as Irish songwriter Paul Kelly sang.

But I just can't see Stephen and his childhood sweetheart Maria breaking up, I just can't see it. They are simply not good-looking enough to part ways at this stage, because they know they won't be able to find someone better. I'm joking. Half-joking. But I do feel that a break-up is close to impossible - they're just one of those couples who weather the inevitable storms. Although you can understand they hurt with all this crybaby business, especially Stephen who comes off as the culprit. He's feeling far worse than I do in a hundred ways, yet full-blown empathy is hard to find when you're really, really hung-over. I promise myself to do my best though.

"Fuck, Steve. This is a baby we're talking about here! Your son! I don't know much about babies, but I know this: they grow the fuck up. He might be feeling strange about you right now for whatever reason, but that won't go on forever. It can't."

"I don't know Jack. The whole situation is freaking me out." Stephen sounds resigned, but at least he's not crying.

"You're giving up too easily." This probably doesn't sound so convincing from a guy who's allergic to relationships, but I'll try it anyway. "You have been a couple for, how long is it now?"

"11 years," Stephen says.

"11 fucking years!" I say, loud enough for everyone in Central Park to hear. "That's history man – that's a serious connection. It's not something you break just by a couple of baby tears."

I smile at my own elegant way with words. This is where I'm at my best, saying what people want to hear, without necessarily believing any of it myself. That's the art of advertising, folks.

I continue: "You're just overwhelmed by the situation. I mean, there's so much stress involved in raising a baby, so much pressure." I don't know where this comes from, but suddenly I'm Doctor Phil, which should work on a softie like Stephen. "I think you and Maria need to spend some quality time together, go on a weekend trip, get a room, eat, shop, drink and fuck. Get back to the basics and find the love. It's there, it's just hidden behind all this baby-pressure."

Stephen's silent. Is he actually listening or just holding back tears? Then from somewhere deep down he speaks.

"Jack, you're a genius. I bet Maria's mother could babysit for a few days and we could go on a short vacation and really get some time together. I can't believe I didn't think about it before, but I guess all I could see was darkness, not solutions. You should've been a psychiatrist or something."

Stephen is now doing the I'm so grateful I'll say anything-routine and I actually appreciate it. I don't know if I'd make a good psychiatrist, though - I like the sound of my own voice, but the never-ending noise of other people's problems would kill me.

We don't need to talk more now. He's feeling better and I want to finish my coffee and meet up with Mike for a chat about my date from hell. So I wish Stephen the best of luck with his angry baby and we say goodbye.

***

My best friend Mike, alias "Cupid", is waiting for me outside our favorite Starbucks on Upper East Manhattan. I'm surprised to find him looking more tired than I do, and I look like road kill. But I'm also very happy to see him, as there's something very comfortable about hanging out with Mike. He's a safe card no matter what mood you're in and a great person to have as a best friend. We don't hang out as much these days because of his dedication to Joanne and the amount of hours I work, but I've managed to wrestle him free for a coffee today. He's of course curious about my blind date with Gwen, a blind date he's more or less responsible for.

Mike is almost always clean and tidy, but today his baby blue shirt is wrinkled, his face has day-old stubble and his gut looks surprisingly soft and doughy. I haven't noticed the weight gain before and it doesn't become him. Belly fat is okay when you're 50, but not before. He needs to take better care of himself and the first weight he should lose is Joanne.

"What hit you?" I ask him, "A train of donuts?"

"Very funny, Jack. I haven't slept that's all. You know I can't sleep when Jo is out with the girls (Joanne's loud and immature friends who I also despise) so I stayed up working all night and now I'm completely exhausted."

You see what I mean? Mike has a heart of gold, but balls of...well, let's say he doesn't have any. I go on the attack.

"You know why you can't sleep when your girlfriend's out? Because you can't trust her, that's why!" I say this too loud and get unwanted attention from a Pakistani-looking hot dog vendor across from us.

"I can trust her. I just worry if she's alright or not."

This is bullshit, but before I tell him what his real worry should be, we enter the doors of the green-white coffee chain. They're making bucks like stars these guys, because it's always packed. The good thing with this coffee shop is that I know my Americano will be made to perfection. Besides, I like the guys behind the counter - they crack me up. "They" are a trio of people from very different backgrounds: Richie - a white rocker dude, Nick - a latino with a gold tooth, and Rhonda - a black woman with a big butt and a laugh that could scare a group of school children from across the street. Together they're always loud, entertaining and constantly throwing jokes at each other's expenses. It might sound like something from a Broadway musical, but it's just how life can be when chemistry finds company.

When Rhonda sees us walk through the door her eyes go big and she shouts, "Ooohhh, here come some extra fine customers! Whaddaya two gentlemen want? You looking fo' some big black lovin? I bet ya'll too weak to handle it," which she accompanies by a satirically sexy pose and a booming laugh. It turns a few heads, but I recognize many as regulars here, so they know it well.

"Nah, Rhon, we're just going to have two blueberry muffins and two coffees and be on our way. Thanks for the offer though." I smile at Rhonda, because how could you not? The woman is a laugh riot.

"Too fancy for our little establishment? I knew it," she says and turns to Richie, who's half-Italian and has more tattoos on his arms than I have hair, and gives him our standard order of one Venti Latte and one Grande Americano. He acknowledges it with a wry smile and starts preparing our coffees. As we take our cups and say goodbye, I feel a bit better already. The hangover has gone from a base drum to a gentle tap, which means I'm slowly but surely recuperating. We head over to the park again, which is starting to get crowded on a fine day like this. A group of Japanese tourists is heading our way, all of them with over-sized baseball caps and cameras hanging from their necks. The world is full of clichés. We spot a nice bench in the middle of the park boulevard and sit down. The sun's beating on our faces and I'm suddenly feeling hot, the alcohol starting to pour from my pores. Mike's already slurping on his coffee – he just loves those lattes. I hate milk myself and would never drink anything you have to stroke out of an animal.

"So, tell me about last night. Gwen's nice, right?" Mike looks like he's expecting me to thank him.

"I bet she's nice if you're old enough to have a hearing aid and can turn it off." I say, immediately putting any misconceptions to rest.

"What? It didn't go well?" Mike's actually shocked. He's a bit like Gwen himself when I think about it - he should date her.

"She almost bored me to death. She's definitely not bad-looking, but when she talks...gaaaah! I wanted to stab her with my cutlery! Always going on and on about her father and her friends. Who gives a fuck? And her voice, it's so horribly nasal it digs a hole down to your brain and starts picking on it like an evil woodpecker. That woman should come with a mute button." I'm exaggerating a bit, it's a characteristic of mine.

Mike's offended. He has this sad kitty look and I'm instantly sorry to disappoint him.

"So what happened?"

"We went to this fancy French place on 52nd street, ate some mediocre miniature food and drank some expensive wine. She yapped on about nothing and I made sounds to acknowledge I was still awake. After a while I couldn't take it anymore and asked her flat out if she wanted to fuck and then we went to my place."

"What?" Mike almost shouts this. I thought Mike knew me and my sometimes less gentlemanly ways.

"You slept with her?"

"Yes, I guess so, I can't remember the details. I think I drank half a bottle of scotch when we got home, got pretty drunk and the rest is hazy. All I know is I woke up next to her snoring like chainsaw. She can't even keep quiet in her sleep, goddammit."

"Wow," he says in disbelief, "I didn't think Gwen was that kind of girl."

This is Mike in a nutshell. He thinks the world is one big yellow submarine and that everyone has good intentions. I admire his positive outlook in a way, but it wouldn't hurt him to be a little less naive.

"Judging from the way she talks, she's not a girl, Mike, she's an old lady. And I've yet to know a girl who will say no to sex just because it's too "early". We're in the 21st century - sex is just sex, it's not a precious gift for women to give up." I'm a strong believer in this and have the record to prove it.

"Well, that's your way of seeing it, Jack. You've been with lots of women (Mike, on the other hand, hasn't), but you usually see the same kind of women. I thought Gwen would be a refreshing change."

"What do you mean the same kind of women? You think I only hook up with stupid girls?" I'm starting to get really annoyed now. I don't have a long fuse and when I'm hung-over it's about half its normal length.

"So you're saying you usually go out with mature and intelligent women? I mean, come on! They're mostly 20-year-old wannabe reality show celebrities. Gwen's a lot more interesting than that."

I know there's some truth to what Mike's saying, but it doesn't mean I like it.

"What the fuck, Mike! I go out with lots of different women! And even so, I'd ten times rather date those hot twenty-somethings than be pussy-whipped by that bitch you live with. If I'm going to get serious with someone I don't want to apologize for breathing, ask for permission to leave the house and spend sleepless nights playing the exciting guessing game called "Is My Girlfriend Sleeping With Other Boys?"."

Suddenly he rises from the bench and says, "Fuck you, Jack. And don't you worry - I'm not going to recommend you to any other women. You're such an asshole, you deserve to be alone."

While Mike races off in anger, I'm again reminded of how fragile he is and how easily provoked I am. I was never good at controlling myself and lately, with my work/age crisis, even less so.

I lean back on the bench and close my eyes, the sun still burning my face. I'll call Mike and apologize later and we'll be fine. We've done this charade before. But I'm starting to worry about what's going on with me, why am I such a dick? My mind has lived a life of its own lately, I'm having strange dreams, sweating more easily during the day, and my breathing is sometimes forced and constricted. Am I going through some kind of middle-age crisis or male menopause? Or is it just my fading career fortunes that are fucking with my head? I sit on the bench for a while, finish my coffee and let my head drift to work. Work, where things aren't going the way they should. Work, where I once was king, but now feel like a ghost.

This makes my headache triple in force, my chest is suddenly tightening and I'm feeling dizzy. I'm almost afraid to stand up, but after a while I manage to and I walk home slowly, step by step, while trying to push the dark thoughts away.

When I get home the apartment is empty and there's a note on the kitchen table. It says: "Call me! xox Gwen :-)" Her number is carefully written below.

Some people have no self-awareness.

***

It's no lie that my job has taken up most of my life and still does. I used to live and breathe advertising and the ad agency I founded six years ago has made me half-famous (in some circles at least), pretty well off financially and maybe also a bit crazy. When I enter the lobby of our prime location office, I almost always feel pride and excitement, because I built this company, I made it what it is.

Or at least what it was.

The agency, my life work, has caused me much happiness and success, a boatload of stress, a pretty grave unwillingness to commit to relationships, and lately also some anxiety. During the years I've sometimes asked myself, is it worth it? Is it worth coming home late at night, eyes red and stomach rumbling after another round of overtime, over and over again? And every single time the answer has been a resounding "Yes!". Nearing my seventh year on overdrive, it's time to ask myself that question again. Will the answer be the same? For once I'm not so sure and it scares the shit out of me. Because if I'm not who I am at work, then who the fuck am I really?

My three-year younger sister thinks I have an unhealthy relationship with work. She says I only care about money, which is a typical thing to come from someone who's desperate to call herself an artist. I don't know if it's the money, fame or success I crave or just a sense of accomplishment, but she's right in saying I'm not the most spiritual, inward-looking guy. We're very different, my sister and I. Raised the same, but very, very different. She's the aspiring artist and I'm the businessman, her New York is not mine. We're talking Brooklyn studio versus Upper East Side penthouse, art exhibitions in the Meat Packing District versus champagne get-togethers in the Hamptons, and flea market searches versus expensive super-brand stores.

Yeah, you wouldn't think we're related.

I'd like to say something about having an "unhealthy" relationship with work. What's unhealthy really? Your career is a BIG part of who you are. When you spend eight or more (a lot more in my case) hours a day, five to seven days a week doing it - you need to do something you care about. You've got to feel passion, commitment, and desire - otherwise it's just waste, right? Are you willing to spend all that time just making a living? Waiting to really live in the weekends? That life isn't for me. So I worked my ass off, saved money, started an agency with my business partner Nicholas and over the years I've made it hugely successful. I wanted to achieve greatness and prioritized accordingly. Relationships were contra-productive to my career. Starting a family wasn't in the equation. Keeping up with friends didn't really make the list - hell I didn't even know who my real friends were! I wanted to hang out with people who could be beneficial to my career and it turns out they wanted the same. It's a scratch my back, I'll scratch yours-world. I'm sometimes thinking how I could've done some things a bit differently and still accomplished great things, and I'm actually surprised some people have decided to stick by me, despite my emotional absence, my fanatic work situation and the person I sometimes become when I don't get my way. I ought to thank my lucky star to have a friend like Mike, but instead I give him shit. Man, I'm sounding negative and sorry for myself. My father always says feeling sorry for yourself is the road paved to hell, advice I've tried to heed all my life. But lately I haven't been so successful.

My own personal road to hell is currently walking through the corridor on the way to my office. I look down at my Blackberry because I don't want to be forced into small talk with my likely disgruntled co-workers. I don't want them to see my discontent and insecurity, and what I'm slowly realizing is fear - the fear of failure.

I manage to raise my head enough to say hi to my loyal secretary and assistant, Angela, before I open the door to my office. Angela has her hair done up in some kind of knot, which is sad, because her hair is maybe her greatest asset. When she lets it out you see how thick, dark and wavy it is, it makes you want to grab it, play with it and run your hand through it. I slept with her once, but I was too drunk and horny to think of running my hand through that beautiful thick mane and I regret that now. The "incident" occurred after a work dinner where I was celebrating a successful campaign, leading to a major account signature, by ordering plenty of shooters. After a while

I was intoxicated enough to see no harm in doing my secretary. She'd just started and I can't really blame her for wanting to bed her boss either - actually I don't disapprove of anyone who wants to sleep with me, I congratulate her on a good choice. Sex is a power thing and women like powerful men. Anyway, we've never spoken a word of what happened between us, which tells me Angela is exactly right for the job. You need a hundred percent professional to trust them with your deepest secrets and I feel I can do that with her.

Stepping inside my large and luxurious office immediately makes me feel a tiny bit better. It's supposed to be the warmest welcome you can get to your workday and it's somewhat comforting it still gives me that feeling, a few years down the road. You see, I was always a sucker for the Wall Street movies, from Gordon Gekko to Patrick Bateman (yeah, although he's a psycho, you've got to admit the guy's got class) and I always wanted a nice Manhattan skyscraper office with floor-to-ceiling panoramic windows, big expensive art on the walls and a large dominating desk, giving you the feeling that here works one of the most powerful men in the city. The view from here, on the 34th floor, is breathtaking. Everything in it is carefully thought out, has a price tag that blows your mind and screams POWER. If you're in a salary discussion with me and you're not intimidated - then I am.

My dream office was designed by my Korean interior designer Kim Song (yeah, that's his real name) after Nicholas referred him to me, following a release party for some new brand of vodka. I don't remember the brand, but I do remember having plenty of it. During the party, I told Nicholas I wanted the best and since he knows pretty much everyone worth knowing in the city, he of course had a guy in his mile-long iPhone contact book who could do the trick. Nicholas is a social beast and a great right hand man for any business, as he hangs out with the New York elite on a day-to-day basis. He sends text messages to Christina Aguilera, plays squash with Matthew Broderick and goes on weekly lunches with Anna Wintour. Nicholas gets our name out and the contracts signed, while I deal with the operations. It's a setup that has worked well. At least until I started to losing my bearings.

So after I got Kim Song's number from Nicholas, I called him up, told him I'd heard he was one of the best in the business and asked him if we could meet up to discuss my new top-of-the-line office. Our initial meeting was really a meeting of minds. I was always impressed by Asian simplicity and neatness, but at the same time I wanted it to be boastful. Not exactly an easy combination to achieve and that's why I needed Kim Song. We started by catalog browsing for materials, inspiration and furniture. At first I had the feeling he was hitting on me, being overly eager to touch my shoulder when we agreed on something, but when I got over that I realized the guy was a true pro and actually pretty much tuned in to what I wanted. In the end he came up with a masculine mix of technology and rustic materials like wood and stone. I can sit in my leather chair, sip on a glass of brandy, watch my Asian stone waterfall and still be able to control all the important functions, from LCD screens to window blinds, with just the touch of a button. And you'll have to look very hard to find a wire.

Describing my office to you makes me think about Nicholas and I realize I haven't seen him in a while. He's always involved in at least five different projects at the same time and doesn't fret half as much as I do over the agency's recent problems to keep major clients. Nicholas was always more of socialite than an advertising man and he probably has enough trust in me to think I can turn the ship around, which is a pretty scary thought for a guy who's at an all-time low on confidence and energy.

Nicholas and I were never close friends outside of work - he has his life and I have mine (which has turned out to be mostly work), but I'm thankful he's my partner because without him, his social networking and supreme ass-kissing skills, we wouldn't have gotten this far. I sometimes wish we had more of a friendship, but on the other hand I don't think Nicholas is as interested in making friends as he's into knowing the right people.

I sit down in my handmade state-of-the-art office chair, which set us back more than most people make in a month's salary and take out my little laptop and turn it on. The computer looks pretty innocent with the glowing apple on it (fruit often does), but lately it hasn't been kind to me. Most e-mails I get these days have some kind of problem in them.

I'm going through my inbox, replying to some, forwarding others and chucking some in the trash, when I find a message which makes my heart stop in its tracks. It seems we're about to lose another one of our biggest clients, a huge moneymaker for us and a soft drink maker for others. The campaign we did for them did not go according to plan, they feel we've abused their brand and they want compensation (we have a "if we don't sell, we'll work for free" guarantee - a great gimmick I came up with, which has now turned out troublesome). I feel my pulse race and then explode. "Fuck!" I shout out to no one and close the laptop lid with a slam. It's quite a smack and something definitely cracks, but right now getting a new computer is the least of my concerns. I spin my chair around and face the wall of windows. This would be a good place to commit suicide and a truly spectacular way to go - just throw myself against the glass. It would turn a few heads, stop some people in the street, make some people's talk for the lunch hour, but then it would fade, the glass would be replaced, a new executive hired, the incident forgotten and New York would move on with its business. I breathe in and out deeply and close my eyes. I need to have a whisky, something, to calm myself down. I turn around and open the left desk drawer to find Bowmore, my liquid friend from Scotland who has helped me still my nerves on numerous occasions. I grab a glass, pour myself a healthy dose and empty it in one sweep. It stings the back of my throat and almost makes my eyes water, but it does the trick - I'm instantly feeling slightly more relaxed. I have another one, thinking I'm like one of those 60's ad executives who always had a few glasses of whisky to get through the day. I understand them completely – the ad game can be pretty unsettling.

My minute of tranquility is disturbed by my phone alarm going off, reminding me it's a day of interviews. We're replacing one of our copywriters and being the control freak I am, I still like to meet all the new people we take onboard, again a testament to this company being a bit like my own personal baby. Besides, I love the interview process as it makes me feel powerful.

I put away the whisky glass and head over to the en-suite bathroom. I rest my hands on the sink and look into the mirror. Still beautiful, still powerful, I tell myself, but honestly, I have a hard time believing it.

***

The first interviewee is Matthew, a young New Yorker with quite an impressive CV. This sadly seems to be the only impressive thing about him and his appearance is the first warning sign. Matthew has a curly patch of dark red hair on his head and freckles all over his baby-ish face. In his over-sized blue suit he looks a bit like a schoolboy in a uniform, which is pretty much exactly what I'm not looking for. I instantly get the feeling Matthew isn't the kind of person who catches the shit before it hits the fan - he scrapes it off afterwards - and during the short interview I have with him, I never really lose that feeling. Matthew's voice is not unsteady, but annoyingly light and his handshake is sweaty and cold. According to the paper in front of me he's 25. I remember when I was 25, I had hair on my handsome face, a stride in my walk and believed the world was to be laid under my feet (I did some of it of course, but mostly ended up laying women). This guy, this half-nerd with unpolished shoes and a nervous laugh, could very well still be a virgin. What that has to do with his job application? Nothing on paper, but plenty in real life. I want to employ tough people, people who know what they want and how to get it. Virgins must have a pretty poor track record of that.

I'd of course love to hire a younger version of myself, as I thought I did the employer a favor by looking for work there. I was cocky, but at least I brought results, passion and hard work to the table.

And in the end that's the only thing every employer wants.

Matthew answers my questions in the way I expected him to - I could probably have written his answers down beforehand. There's nothing original or interesting about him, which is strange for a guy who's looking for a job as a writer. Some of his work is competent his portfolio tells me, but I'm looking for a future star, someone who can unleash award-, and most importantly, account-winning ideas, not a person who's decent and happy to get a job, any job in the industry. And although he might have a slice of talent hidden under his red hair, he'll need to be talented somewhere else. Matthew's in the middle of a sentence when I thank him for his time and tell him I'll be in touch. He looks surprised by the rudeness of this, but if he's done his research properly, he shouldn't be, and if he didn't, well...fuck him. I'm not known for silky hands and Matthew's lack of balls makes me angry. I know it takes a while to find a good writer, but I've got no patience for these things anymore - I just want to get it over with. I drink another scotch before Angela calls in the next candidate, but it doesn't really help to dissipate my anger.

As I could've predicted, the following two interviews are even more depressing than the first one. What's wrong with people these days? Either creative director Jim has been smoking some strong herbs or the applicants must have sugared their résumés like donuts. I can feel my mood darkening and I shout out to Angela over the intercom to get me a second Americano to balance out the alcohol heating up my blood. I haven't had any food today and I need to get both lunch and some fresh air to function properly, but I have one more interview to get through before I can head out.

I look down at the next CV in the pile in front of me and I actually remember liking this one when I skimmed through these papers last week. Mindy Wallace wrote the best and most creative cover letter I've seen in a while and her portfolio isn't bad. And I have a feeling that if she can win me over in written form, she could also do it in the interview.

After a while Angela comes in with another cup of coffee, accompanied by a skinny dark-haired girl with a Mediterranean looking face, an olive skin tone (she looks to hail more from Italy than Kansas) and a nice light-grey business dress. She's definitely attractive and my mood lifts immediately. A promising start. I stand up, say hi, and greet her with my biggest smile and point to the chair in front of my desk. She has a confident air about her - she knows she has a good chance at this job and I like that. Optimism, no matter if it's misguided or just, is far more flattering than nerves.

It doesn't take me long to realize Mindy is the one. That's how it usually happens, after a while you just know. So I offer her the job on the spot, but I also try to save a little money by aiming for a salary lower than we really should pay her, considering the market value of the position, her previous experience, and so on. I study her face for a reaction. She has nice features, slim and angular, a bit like a matinee movie star. While I watch her, part of me expects her to burst into a smile and reach over and shake my hand. This is what I want to happen here, what ought to happen. I've had enough of a bad day already and prefer to get this over and done with so I can have lunch. But Mindy surprises me. Her eyes turn slightly downward in disappointment and she says she'll think about it.

Something snaps inside of me.

"Think about it?" I scream in her face. "What is there to think about? You come to one of the best agencies in New York (not really sure about this anymore), get an offer only an idiot would refuse and you tell me you'll think about it?" I inadvertently spit at her when I say this. Mindy looks at me big-eyed now, terrified like a deer in the headlights of a car. Who wouldn't be? Who'd expect this kind of tirade? But she composes herself, lifts her eyes from the ground, looks straight into mine and says with an impressive calm:

"I'd kind of thought you'd offer me more money."

I know I shouldn't take offense, but this is a rejection to me and I can't take rejections. It means Mindy knows her own value, she might have other interviews lined up, possibly even other offers to consider. I'm caught in the act of the cheapskate and I've got no way out but to bluff, to attack when she least expects it. Sometimes it's good to drink during office hours.

"Money? You think this is about money? I give you a bright future on a silver plate and you start talking about money? This agency is about passion, about pushing your own limits and the true art of advertising. It's the best fucking place to work in the industry and you know that. And we can pay you well - after you show you're worth it."

I give out a chuckle and look away, like I can't stand to look at her right now.

"I...", she stumbles.

"You know what?" I say in my tough guy negotiation voice, "I could tell you right now to get the fuck out of my office, it would be as easy as one-two-three. But for some reason I'm going to give you one more chance to say yes. Say yes or leave now." I give her a look telling her I mean business and I'm the one holding the cards. This is not true, because I'm tired of interviews and I really hope she takes the job, but I need to stick to my gambit.

"I guess I take the job," Mindy says, sounding more confused than happy.

I turn on my brightest smile (I know I'm acting like a complete lunatic here), stretch out my hand and say, "Welcome! I promise you you'll love it here. You can sort out the details with Ellen over at HR, I'll drop her an e-mail. Now please get out of my office." When Mindy leaves, she's probably as confused as I am after what just took place. I take a long look at her ass and reach for the bottle of scotch in my desk drawer and take a healthy sip, straight from the bottle.

I'm losing it. Seriously.

***

I go for lunch with my friend (acquaintance might be a better word) Russell at an Italian restaurant which is more expensive than nice. The prices are in fact ridiculously high, the service pretty nonchalant and the food varies from delicious to decent. But many celebrities go here and of course all the wanna-see and wanna-be celebs too. I'm no celebrity myself, not unless you're in advertising or read business magazines from two years ago, but I like to be around them. It makes me feel special. And I've got the money to eat here, which is good, because all this place wants is my money and plenty of it.

Russell is half-an-hour late as usual and I've already emptied two glasses of a 200-dollar bottle Amarone Italian wine when he arrives in his professional attire: a dark-grey suit, white shirt and pink tie. He even put time into gelling and combing his chestnut hair backwards, making him look more like a Wall Street shark than a real estate broker. This is in stark contrast to his casual attire, which basically consists of things homeless people wouldn't wear. Russell is a self-championed fashionista who mixes and misses more than he matches. He's always out of place and therefore always stands out, which is what he wants, of course.

"Fuck man," I say loudly and point to my Rolex Submariner as soon I see him nearing our table. A Gwyneth Paltrow look-alike at the table next to us gives me a look.

Russell looks guilty. He knows he fucked up. Again.

"Let me take a moment to teach you how time works, Russell. You see this watch here? You see how the small arrow is moving and the bigger arrows are still? Well, the bigger arrows move too! And they move especially fast when you're about to be somewhere at a said time."

"Sorry man," Russell says, "had a slow client."

"You sold anything?"

"No signed papers yet, but yes, I think so. They're an older New York couple who moved to Florida a few years ago, got tired of the gated communities and people reversing without looking and now want to get back to the big city. Jack and Jill - can you believe that's actually their real names? I showed them a townhouse on Upper West Side which isn't very modern, but it's spacious and good value if you do it up properly, and the look on their faces told me it's pretty much a done deal."

To be fair, Russell doesn't have to work much. Property in New York sells itself and through his father's agency he has enough contacts to always have wealthy clients knocking on his door, ready to pay a hefty sum for a slice of the Big Apple. Russell only has to show them where the slice is and take quite a piece for himself.

"So I think I have a buyer for lunch today?" I say. Paying for lunch is good compensation for being late.

"Sure," Russell says, flashing me his breadwinner smile.

My friendship with Russell is simple on the border of mundane, meaning Russell is like a Homo Erectus in a suit. We're mostly drinking and lunching buddies and rarely meet without an unhealthy dose of alcohol, although I always seem to be around alcohol these days. He's younger, more energetic, and still very much in the fast lane of things. We're probably too alike to be closer friends, the difference being that, while I worked my ass off to get here, he got everything pretty much served on a silver plate. This might sound like I'm jealous, and yes, sometimes I am.

Most of our conversations revolve around things we like to buy or women we like to bone, which is Russell's caveman expression for it. We don't really discuss politics, sports, or any other topics, except for maybe real estate. It's a shallow friendship and it would bore me to death to hang out with him on a more permanent basis, but for hitting the nightclubs he's the best friend you can get. I always had a natural talent for meeting women, but Russell's one level above me, he's born for it.

I tell Russell about Mindy, concentrating on the hotness and not the breakdown I had in the end of the interview, as I'm still trying to figure out what the hell happened there.

"She sounds interesting. I like the dark hair. Kansas girl, you say? Reminds me of Nicki, you know that girl with the boyish haircut? Fantastic body and crazy as a coked-up rabbit in bed. We had some good times. Why don't you invite this Mindy out for a drink?"

"I don't know man, I've been there, done that. I don't sleep around with people at work anymore."

Russell looks to the side, over at the Paltrow look-alike and says "true", but I can tell he's not really listening. This kind of common sense wisdom is very difficult to impart on a shallow brain like Russell's. He picks up his glass, sniffs the wine and looks at me and says: "Well, if you don't want her, maybe you can set me up?"

I quickly regret having mentioned Mindy, as Russell's hornier than a Viagra-popping rabbit. He's one of those guys who writes every girl down in a notebook and rates her. But he wouldn't admit it to me, as I think he still looks up to me somewhat.

I want to stop where this conversation's going and say: "Yeah, we'll see. Maybe." And then I change the subject to Russell's new Bugatti. It's not a very interesting topic and I soon realize how bored I am with guys like Russell - they never have anything interesting or important to say, and today, for whatever reason, Russell seems more distracted than usual and doesn't get into his somewhat entertaining, "girls I slept with recently"-routine. Instead he keeps thumbing away on his iPhone from time to time. We finish our octopus angel-hair pasta and the bottle of wine and when we've left the restaurant he says:

"Did you see Gwyneth Paltrow over there? Man, she's still hot!"

***

It's seven o'clock and I haven't had anything to eat except a Snickers bar since my lunch with Russell. I need food and I don't feel like eating alone. I run through my options.

Stephen's out of the question. I don't want to hang out with people who have bigger problems than me - the person needs to cheer me up, not the other way around. Mike's stapled to Joanna and I'm 99 percent sure he won't be able to come, so I'm not even going to bother calling him. Russell again? No way, I got enough of him at lunch. Don't I have any more close friends? Can I really count them on one, feeble hand? Wow, that's kind of... sad.

Then I come to think of Karen, my sister, who I haven't talked to in weeks, although she lives in the same city. My little sister and I don't have a very good brother-sister relationship and I think part of her actually resents me for never being the caring big brother I ought to have been because of my one-track mind focused on success. I don't really know if Karen needed any brotherly assistance though, like our mother she grew up to be pretty tough and independent in a family where everyone's his or her own island. The Reynolds were never Family Ties material (you know that show with a young Michael J. Fox where everybody says they love each other all the time?), we were all occupied working on our own projects, hobbies and careers, something that of course meant there was little quality family time. I'm actually not really sure what family time means.

I never thought about these things until my mother passed away four years ago from lung cancer. 40 years of smoking at least one pack of cigarettes a day did that to her and in the end her throat was red like a stop sign, and the cancer looked you right in the face as you talked to her.

I actually thought my mother's fight with cancer would bring the family together, because death should do that, right? But although we all cried, drank and talked about her, we quite casually went on with our lives afterwards. My father moved from his beloved Boston to start a new life in Miami and Karen and I stayed in New York, where we quickly drifted apart again.

I have recently started to wish we were different.

"Hi sis!" I say, trying to sound energetic.

"Hi," Karen's voice is low and slightly wooden, I can tell she didn't expect this call, but that doesn't mean she's overjoyed about it either.

"So, what's up? Painting?" I sound stupid of course. This timid, "what are you doing"-talk, is not really me and my sister knows it.

"No, I'm waiting for Dylan. We're going to watch a movie."

Dylan is Karen's band-playing emo-boyfriend (you know, guys who think life is against them from the start, listen to depressive music and try to cover their face with hair), and I can't stand guys who play in bands. He's far from the type of dude I'd hang out with, which means he's probably a good match for Karen.

"What are you watching?"

"A Spanish drama, not really something you'd like." Karen's right, she knows I'm not very interested in small European films.

"Aha, okay. I just wanted to check on you. Everything's good?" I'm grasping at straws here - the idea of the loving and caring brother is something I could have sold ten years ago maybe. Not now.

"Yeah, I guess. I sold a painting a few days ago, through my blog. It's great to get some extra money. And Dylan got a few more gigs."

These gigs are usually played at half-empty bars in out of way-locations and I'm pretty sure Dylan isn't destined towards musical greatness, but what do I know?

"Okay, that's good. Progress!"

The word progress is a heritage from my father, his life motto and the one word he really wanted us to believe in.

"Yep, some progress, I guess," Karen says.

"You heard from dad?"

Our father is a standard item of our conversations. Neither Karen nor I are good at calling him though and he's not world champion at staying in touch with us either.

"We talked, let's see, maybe three weeks ago? He told me about his new girlfriend, a girl he's been seeing for a few months now. She's young, about my age and her name is Melody. Can you believe that? It's probably some porn star or something."

Karen's obviously disgusted by the thought of our father dating girls half his age, but he has always been a ladies man and he's good looking for being 60 with this "permanent" tan (he has his own tanning bed in the basement), a good physique and a thick wallet. So I'm not really surprised he's met someone named Melody.

In the background I hear a door slam. It's probably Dylan, back from a "gig".

"Ha-ha," I laugh, "you know how dad is. You got me curious now, I should call and check on him."

"You do that, Jack. I'm going to start watching this movie now, but we can talk some other time, okay?"

"Yeah, yeah, sure. I'll call you. Take it easy, sis."

"Sure, I will. Bye."

"Bye."

The silence after that bye is a long silence. I don't know what I'd hoped for, but grabbing a beer with my sister wouldn't have been too shabby.

I look up at the sky and feel the first drops of rain hit my shoulder. Around me people are rushing off to their after-work beers, homes, wives, kids, dogs, roommates, and I'm standing on the pavement holding my cellphone hard like it's the only friend I've got. I must be extremely lonely, because in the end I actually decide to call Russell anyway, as he's the only guy I can think of who would be free to have a drink on such short notice.

"Yo," Russell replies.

"Hi," I say. "Drinks?"

"No time for that, bro. Got a date."

"A date? Why didn't you tell me at lunch?"

"Didn't know about it then." Russell says, sounding stressed.

"So you just scheduled a date in the afternoon? How did that happen? You walked into someone in the street?"

I say this but think: Shit, this guy is good!

"Yeah, pretty much. No time for details now. Got to go."

Russell's ready to hang up - he apparently has better places to be than talking to me.

"Okay. Talk later then."

"See ya."

Click.

So here I am alone. Everybody's watching movies, saving marriages, and dating while I'm walking around the city in a slight drizzle with a headache and a rumbling belly. I can't recall feeling this miserable in a long time. The rain's pouring heavier by the minute and I look at the sky in disbelief. I need to get under a roof and run across the street and into a Borders bookstore. I haven't been in a bookstore in a long time. Although they're not really bookstores anymore, they're social interaction centers serving coffee and muffins, which is good, because I'm starving.

I walk upstairs to the Borders café and look around. People are scattered about at small tables, playing with their iPads, typing on their laptops, sharing a coffee or reading a book. It looks like such a lonely place I instantly feel even more depressed.

I stand in line behind an old man in a tweed jacket. He emits a rancid smell and I'm trying to block my nostrils and focus on what sandwich I want instead. Suddenly I'm at the front of the line, but the pimple-faced and pig-nosed girl taking my order doesn't exactly raise my spirits. I order a chicken cranberry baguette, a bottle of still water and a large Americano. I pay and move to the side for my seventh coffee of the day.

The wait is longer than usual for just an Americano and I'm starting to feel impatient when the pig-nosed girl shows up again. With a Cappuccino.

"I ordered an Americano," I say, holding up my lactose-infested cup for her to see. "They don't contain milk." I give her a stern look.

"Oh. I heard you say Cappuccino," she says.

The pig's apparently deaf and uninformed about the phrase "the customer is always right". I sigh loudly.

"I said Grande Americano. Now can you please just get me one."

"Ok," she says, clearly annoyed and snatches the cup from my hands so fast the cup tumbles over and a sliver of coffee spills out through the breathing hole (because you can't really drink from that hole) and onto my hand. The piping hot coffee burns my fingers and stains my blue Dolce Gabbana shirt.

"Fuck!" I cry out.

"Oh, I'm so sorry, sir!" The pig's frantic now. "Sorry, it just slipped out of my hands."

"I think your job just slipped out of your hands," I say, while trying to wipe the coffee off of my shirt.

"I'm going to talk to your manager about this," I continue, squeezing out what could likely be the lamest line of all time. Still, like a reflex, I say it.

I feel the whole room looking at me, but the heart-breaking silence is soon replaced with the background noise of thunder and even heavier rain hitting the window, and that's kind of the drop, if you excuse the pun.

It's the second time that day I want to jump through a window, but instead I sit down with my stained shirt and my tasteless baguette and just soak in all the self-pity and loathing.

***

The next day at work I find the new employee, Mindy, in the company lobby. She looks excited and she should be. Maybe the success of getting a job with us has sunken in. She rises from the chair and I stretch out my hand.

"Good morning, Molly," I say, intentionally the wrong name. She has to understand how hard she needs to fight to win my respect.

"Mindy," she corrects me. She's slightly offended I didn't remember it. Good.

"My assistant Angela will set you up with everything you need, take 15 minutes to look through the company manual - that's our bible, the IT-guys will provide you with a new computer and we'll have Jim over there - I point to the young and red-headed creative director I got very cheaply two years ago - will give you all the background and briefs you need to get started." I look her in the eyes and smile.

Then from somewhere deep down in Desperation Land, I say this:

"I suggest you and I have lunch. Let's meet 12:15 outside the office. I'll have Angela reserve a table for us." I say this, but I don't really know why I'm saying it. It just struck me as a good idea all of a sudden. Maybe it's Mindy's looks that's doing this to me, because she's absolutely stunning today in a black mid-length business skirt and a white shirt, or maybe I'm just lonely.

"Sounds good," Mindy says, but I'm pretty sure it doesn't.

***

Before my lunch with the attractive, but likely confused Mindy, I have a very important client meeting with the angry soft drink company who made my heart stop earlier. The campaign we did for them was a fiasco and ended up costing them a small fortune with nothing to show for it. The sales are down and the surveys they've conducted show their customers didn't like it. We screwed up and they're right to blame us. It wasn't a very inspired project for some reason and I should maybe have been more in control, but I can't really remember when I was in control last.

But there's no point in dwelling in the past, now I need to save our asses and make the fizzy fuzzy people believe they'll win in the long run. My first job, therefore, is to explain to their chief marketing officer, Brian Anderson, that we're not yet in the long term and it will take more campaigns and more work to get the brand and sales boost we promised. I have my work cut out for me, because you can't really explain patience to marketing people. It's all in the numbers.

The meeting's ugly, Brian's ugly and Brian's furious. His face is pink from all the screaming he's been doing and together with his curly, blond hair it makes him look a bit like a giant, angry baby who someone forgot to feed.

Brian's been "kind" enough to bring his laptop and we're looking at before-and-after figures, once approved TV commercials and the tagline they've now realized aren't aligned with their brand platform. He goes on to shout in my face that they're thinking of suing us. But you can't really sue someone for doing a bad job can you? Well, this is America so who knows?

My head's spinning and I need oxygen. Brian isn't giving me any, although I'm doing my best to sound understanding, when what I really want to do is punch him in the face. But I can't, because it's not what professionals do and although my track record of professionalism hasn't been great lately, I desperately need to be on my best behavior here. So I tell him, in a nice way, that I find it odd he thinks there are a lot of problems with our ideas, ideas he and the rest of the soft drink people first thought fantastic.

This results in more shouting in my face and I'm sure Brian's face is bound to pop like a ripe zit. But it doesn't and when he's calmed down we agree that according to contract and our sales message, we'll do the next campaign for free, as compensation for the bad results. I agree to this because I really need Brian and his company. Losing the account could be the final nail in our coffin.

When Brian's followed out by Angela he throws a typical asshole remark, just before saying goodbye. He says, "make sure you get it right this time," and then turns around to give me his fake, fat-faced smile. He knows he won this battle and he's smug about it too. I briefly picture myself running after him and kicking him in his chubby ass, but it's just a fantasy. Brian is today's winner and I just need to make sure I don't need to see his red face in my office ever again. It's sad in a way that an idiot like Brian can be in charge of something so important in such a big and successful company, but that's how it goes in this business, or in any business - you don't exactly need to be the great Lord Nelson to be steering the ship.

When our tense and disturbing meeting is over, I'm exhausted and broken. My hands are shaking and my face is burning. Not a great preamble to my lunch date.

***

Mindy's quiet during our walk to the restaurant. I'm not really in a talking mood either after my fight with the red-faced retard. I need a hardcore drink to clear my head. I of course also understand her reluctance to shoot the breeze - I must've made quite an impression for all the wrong reasons. I don't want to apologize though, because I prefer to be intimidating than to come off as a nutcase with a temper problem, which might be closer to the truth.

I try to ask her some random personal questions to loosen her up, to at least get on talking terms. How does she like New York, does she have any hobbies, and so on. She says she's into yoga (which spells "limber body" to me), she likes to read books and has two chubby cats living with her. Cats are the sign of lonely women, so I feel slightly hopeful she's single and approachable. There's nothing better than women to take my mind of myself.

As this is a kind of date in my twisted mind, we go to one of my favorite American Noveau restaurants. I want to impress Mindy and the splendid mix of French and Italian food, along with a spectacular goose liver pate, should do the trick. Angela has booked us my favorite window table and as we sit down I immediately order two pre-lunch Martinis. God knows I need at least one.

"Sorry, but I'd rather just drink water." Mindy laughs nervously at the proposal of starting her first working day with a cocktail. She's obviously a rookie.

"But it's only one drink! And we're celebrating!" I give her what can maybe be interpreted as a crazy look, unintentionally so.

Mindy's surprised by my sudden change in moods - from asshole to suitor in one go.

"What are we celebrating?" she says.

"That you joined us of course! It's a welcome in liquid form. All good things come in liquid form." I chuckle at my own joke, which is bad and makes me sound like an alcoholic. And it's dawning on me that it might actually be true.

"Yes, but I want to stay alert during the first day and I'm not really good at handling alcohol," Mindy says.

"But it's only one drink," I beg, now a bit excited by the possibility she might not be able to handle it.

"Thanks, but no thanks," Mindy says, sounding a little irritated by my nagging.

"Ok," I say grumpily, "that means one more for me."

I should have guessed Mindy was going to be a sober bore. She had some of the characteristics and it also fitted in with my recent streak of bad luck.

I decide to drink anyway and forget about my dreamed-up chances of lunchtime intercourse. Mindy's locked up like a clam and as soon as I try to get a bit private with her she crawls back into her shell. It's good to be professional, but it can really be a buzz-kill as well. Mindy's closed-ness sadly leads me to be the narcissist I can be and I end up talking about myself for basically the entire lunch. Mindy stays polite and pretends to listen to everything and deep down I feel so lonely I actually appreciate her bored company.

Problem is, I soon get a little too intoxicated for my own good. I'm on my third glass of wine (to add to the two martinis) when I suddenly get the feeling I desperately need her to open up a bit for us to get just a little closer. So I cross the line and ask her if she has a boyfriend. It doesn't come out as casually as it was intended and she looks a bit taken aback, but says yes, she has, his name is Todd and they're engaged.

I make a disappointed slur and finish my third glass of wine. "Shame on a fine girl like you. We could've really hit it off." I look out the window. It's a sunny day and yet I feel like it's raining on me.

Mindy must be shocked at my audacity. I've broken every rule in the book and she's likely considering some kind of legal action. She drinks her water and looks like she wants the glass to swallow her and spit her out as far away from me as possible.

I know how she feels.

Somehow I manage to save myself from further embarrassment and we walk silently back towards the office when my phone rings. I don't recognize the number, so I pick up.

It's Gwen. She wonders if I want to have dinner with her tonight and if I feel like sushi. I'm so shocked by her calling me again after I clearly ditched her, I can't say anything but yes. I don't know how it happens, but I guess being slightly drunk, confused and desperate for company helps. She says she will take care of the booking and I only need to be outside Kurumas on 47th street at eight. I've heard great things about the place, so although I don't know how I'm going to take another night of Gwen's brainless talking, a sushi dinner with her sounds far better than a delivery pizza alone in my penthouse.

***

I regret agreeing to this date with Gwen as soon as I lay eyes on her. We're meeting outside the restaurant and a blind person could tell she has her expectations up. In contrast to my jeans and wrinkled black shirt, she's wearing a dress more fitting for the red carpet than a second dinner date with a guy who doesn't even care enough to iron his shirt. I should be flattered by her effort, but right now I need to put my strength into not throwing up. It's not Gwen's fault, she's not that bad, it's just a feeling that came over me in the afternoon and which has been increasing in force.

"You look fantastic," I manage to say.

"Thanks!" she says and kisses me on the cheek as we hug hello. I hate cheek kisses, but Gwen's the kind of girl who wouldn't greet another person without one.

As soon as I enter the doors of the stylish Japanese restaurant, I'm feeling hot. I don't know why, the conditioned air inside is cool, but for some reason there's a fire going on inside of me. A neatly dressed waitress with a soft voice shows us to a small wooden table and as I sit down I feel a drop of sweat curl down my spine. I look at Gwen who seems happy and more confident than last time we met. God knows why. She might sense something's off with me though, as she takes the commando to order a bottle of Chardonnay and sparkling water. I don't object, as I'm more concerned with what's going on with my body than with what kind of alcohol I'm going to drink.

Gwen isn't as talkative today, something I'd appreciate more if I didn't feel dizzy and had a small ant-farm running around inside my left arm.

I down the first glass of wine fast, hoping for relief, but nothing happens. Instead, my whole left side feels numb. Gwen's giving me looks from time to time, like she's starting to think there's something wrong with me.

I'm starting to think so too.

When the first plate of sushi rolls arrives, my heartbeat's pounding, my vision's blurring and I'm feeling drops of sweat on my forehead. I'm trying to focus my eyes on something, but can't.

"Jack, are you alright?" I hear Gwen say from a distance. I stand up in an attempt to go to the bathroom, but as I'm rising from my chair I feel the legs fold under me and I crash down like a fighter plane. My head hits the floor with a thud and all is dark.

***

My eyes adjust to the light. My head's throbbing and my mouth is in the Sahara. Am I dead? I wish. Straight in front me, looking at me and still wearing her fancy dress, is Gwen. It hits me like a fist to the face: I'm in a hospital bed.

"Jack!" She says like I just came out of a cake.

"Hi," I croak.

"How do you feel?"

I'm fantastic! I feel like saying, but I lack the energy and settle for, "I've been better. What happened?"

"I don't know, you just fainted. I couldn't figure out what the hell happened to you. It was scary. Thankfully the ambulance was pretty fast in getting you here."

"Can you get me a doctor or a nurse, please?" I say.

When Gwen leaves the room, I'm feeling like I'm about to throw up. I close my eyes again and think: well this is a new low, but only a few seconds later I hear a voice which wakes me up from my self-pity.

"Mr. Reynolds, Mr. Reynolds, how are you feeling?" I open my eyes and see a very big round head with thick glasses on it, a Doctor Potato head.

"Thirsty," which also means: how do you think I feel? I'm in a hospital for God sakes! It seems like people in hospitals ask the most stupid questions.

"Here's some water for you," says Gwen and hands me a bottle of Evian from her purse. The doctor's still studying me, his round head bobbing up and down like it was floating on water. He might have Parkinson's.

"We can't see anything seriously wrong with you, Mr. Reynolds. Blood pressure a bit high, but other than that you seem okay. But I've seen things like this before, although it's rare the person faints. I think you had some kind of anxiety attack, which usually derives from stress and trauma. Is this something you recognize in your life?"

"I don't know really. I've not really had any major traumas in my life. My mother died a few years ago, but I don't think I reacted that badly to it. Hmm, that sounded bad, I mean I think I handled it pretty well."

The doctor looks at his notepad and jots something down. He's taking notes. Is he some kind of shrink? It seems like I need one.

"Well, the passing of family members can come up later in life and affect you harder than you first thought. Anything other than that? Have you been under severe stress lately? At work or in your private life?"

I don't really know how to answer. What's severe stress? I've been stressed most of my working life, I thought it was normal.

"I guess. I work under a lot of stress of course."

"Then it's not unlikely your body has reached the limit of what it can take, Mr. Reynolds. This is something which could've been building up for years. Have you been feeling any numbness of limbs? Pressure in the chest?"

"Yes, both." The doctor jots down another note. I'm curious about what he's writing. Or maybe he's playing Sudoku.

"Mr. Reynolds, I'd suggest you take this thing very seriously. Stress can play nasty tricks on the body. This should be a warning sign for you to work less and I'd recommend you to take some time off and just try to relax and rest as much as possible. If you want to see a psychologist and don't already have one, I can recommend someone for you. Let me write his number down." Dr. Potato head writes some more and continues, "I'm going to give you a subscription for some pills that can help lower your heart rate and calm you down if you start feeling symptoms like these again. We get a lot of people here with extreme stress issues these days, so there's nothing uncommon or strange about this. But remember, nothing's worth risking your life over. Not even work."

He gives me the note and smiles at me like I was a kid being handed a lollipop. I look down at the note and see...nothing really, because like most doctors he has horrible handwriting, which at least means we have something in common.

I'm dazed and confused but manage to squeeze out a thank you. I'm still shocked by how fragile I am. I usually never even catch a cold and all of a sudden I fall apart like this? Do I really need to see a therapist? It would be another big blow to my already shaky ego.

This and many other thoughts are tumbling around in my head while Gwen takes me home in a cab. My legs are jelly and I'm tired beyond words, but Gwen's remarkably good support in what must surely have been the worst date of her life. It's probably weak consolation it was my worst too.

***

It's morning. Gwen's just gone off to work after I've assured her a thousand times I'm fine. But of course I'm not fine. I feel like there's a black hole inside of me, growing and sucking the rest of me in, piece by piece. I'm completely drained of energy, but I can't even have my morning espresso, because Gwen said it might bump my heart rate up. I've gone from attractive advertising mogul to frail senior citizen in one night.

I think about Gwen. What would I have done without her? She took me to hospital, brought me home, took care of me, and spent the night here just because she was worried. I didn't even call her back after our first date and she does all these nice things for me. But despite how great she's been to me, I don't want her to think this is a pathway into some kind of relationship, because it isn't. I don't know if I can do relationships. At least not until I start loving myself again.

But if I've hit rock bottom, then things can only go up, right? The question is how I turn it around. That's what I need to figure out. The doctor wanted me to take a vacation and maybe it's not such a bad idea, because I haven't had a proper one in years. But where to go and what to do? Traveling alone doesn't sound very exciting at the moment and none of my friends would be able to tag along either.

Then a rare thought enters my head: dad. I haven't seen him since Christmas, when he came on his yearly visit, and although we're not close, he usually has a refreshing way of dealing with setbacks and plenty of positive energy to rub off on me.

So in not more than a flimsy heartbeat, I've decided to seek my father's help and pay a visit to his home in Coral Gables, outside Miami.

***

My father's name is Hank, named after the legendary country singer Hank Williams, who my grandmother was deeply in love with back in the days. He was born and raised in Boston and lived there practically all his life, until his ex-wife, vis-á-vis my mother, died. That made him sell his house, pack his bags and leave for the sunny weather and the nice golf courses of a quaint and beautiful city outside Miami called Coral Gables. My father was probably one of the most successful realtors in the Boston area and he in many ways made me who I am, a business-minded workaholic, as he always worked very hard and was desperate to instill the same values in me.

The love for hard work was also the most common trait between him and my mother. They were obsessively dedicated and busy all the time and if that kind of focus brought them together, it's also what tore them apart.

Their drive and ambition also hindered them from developing great parenting skills and that's why we had Clara. Clara was the nanny, cook, and cleaner of the house and was paid to allow my parents to focus on their careers. But my sister and I always felt there was a lot more than money to our relationship - Clara genuinely loved us as her own.

She never became a real mother though. When she took the job and joined our family she was already in her early fifties and lived alone. Karen once asked her why she didn't have kids, considering how good she was with us, but the question seemed to sting her and she just bit her lip and said, "Because it's not the way God intended it, dear." She looked up and her eyes were empty and distant. After a long pause she finished her thought, "But I have you, so I guess he blessed me some other way."

Despite God never granting her children of her own, Clara was a strong believer and used to go to church every Sunday. She sometimes took a break in the day to pray and you could find her on her knees in one of the rooms in the house, her eyes closed, her hands clasped together, her mouth moving quietly.

But as strong as her faith was, she sometimes looked so sad and lonely and I remember thinking there was something dark and troubled inside of her I wanted to save her from.

That darkness turned out to be cancer. When we were getting too old to have a nanny, Clara's God played a lousy trick on us and gave her colon cancer, and if there was a time in my life where sadness washed down on me like a hailstorm, it was when Clara's life powers slowly crawled out of her. I went to the hospital every day during her sickness, although it hurt me so bad to see her fade away. Because that's what cancer does to you, it sucks all the life out of you and shrinks you.

I didn't see her die though. I got to know second hand when my mother gathered us in the living room to give us the "heartbreaking and dreadful news". I remember her crying, which was rare - words coming out staccato style, each syllable stumbling onto one another, every word jumping out abruptly and falling dead to the floor. She knew how much Clara meant to us and in the back of her mind she must have felt that the bond we had with Clara was something special, even more special than the bond we had with her, our own mother.

I hid in my room for hours afterwards. I locked the door, didn't come out for supper. Instead I snuck out of the house when everybody was asleep and just walked the streets. It felt like someone was squeezing my intestines together and I've never felt anything like it since, not even when my own mother died.

After Clara's death we landed into something of a dark age in the Reynolds family. My mother and father started fighting a lot more while both Karen and I were entering a difficult phase, two youngsters bereft of our guardian. This should perhaps have been a good time to stick together and develop a strong brother-sister relationship, but it just didn't happen. I started staying out late nights with my friends, my grades were dropping and I felt terribly confused between my parent's newfound hatred for each other and my emotional debris after Clara's death.

In the end it was my father who picked me up and turned me around, and I'm pretty sure that's why we became closer than my mother and I ever got. He realized their fighting wasn't leading anywhere except to an inevitable divorce and I was the one suffering the most. So he decided to give me the greatest gift he could, his time, which meant he sat down and pushed me through homework, followed up on who my friends were, how I was doing in school, took me out fishing and other father-son activities. He really wanted to make sure I did something with my life and I'm thankful he saw the potential. He told me stories which had inspired him when he was younger, everything from railroad tycoons to Wall Street sharks and although I don't remember many of them, I remember the feeling they brought me, the urge and drive to succeed.

But although my father made me who I am, it's my mother I've been thinking about lately, mostly in an effort to try and understand her and why I have the feeling she never really enjoyed having kids. Don't get me wrong, she loved us in her own little way, but maybe it was more something she felt she had to do, rather than something she really wanted for herself. I don't want to label my mother as a mean person though, because she wasn't, far from it. In fact, she was very generous and loved working with charity - I can't even name half of the projects or organizations she was involved in (it was basically rights for everyone, all the time!), but somehow she just couldn't get into the role of a mother. Maybe in the end she wanted to do these things to compensate for not being the parent she should have been.

My mother took the divorce well. Within a year she met a doctor at a conference and soon remarried and moved to Wisconsin. Karen stayed with my father while I was already on my way to New York, happy not to hear another argument between my parents.

I went to university in the Big Apple and a few years later Karen followed suit, although I studied communication and she the arts.

We talked occasionally over the phone, my mother and I, but the divide was too big for us to really connect. It's hard to explain how it feels not being able to talk to your own mother on an emotional level, but that's how it was and I've slowly come to realize how it has shaped my life. I don't need a psychologist to tell me my distrust in women, in myself with women and in relationships in general, stems from my childhood and my strange relationship with my mother.

Anyway, when I was doing great strides in my career, working 60-hour workweeks and starting to grow the agency, cancer again visited our family when my mother found out she had lung cancer. It went incredibly fast after that, and when I saw her next, she didn't have much time left.

I was surprised to see my father cry at her funeral. I had never seen him cry before and even though I was tear-eyed myself, I didn't expect him to air his emotions like that.

After the funeral the three remaining Reynolds sat in the empty hotel bar in our four-star Milwaukee hotel and had a few drinks together. The mood was somber and my father's eyes were hollow like the grave they recently put his ex-wife in. He hadn't said as much as a word all day and although he wasn't a big talker, you could see how the pain held him back. Karen looked lost and out of place and I was constantly on my phone trying to solve problems at work. When I hung up and sat down my father said:

"I'm sure gonna miss your mother. We had some very nice years together and I bet she shared a happy time with Bob (the doctor) too. But let me tell you one thing. I know your mother as well as anyone and I know the only thing she would want us to do right now is to go on with our lives. We mourn her, of course, but death is a part of life and there's a time for grief and a time for moving on and that's what your mother would've wanted us to do as quickly as possible."

Neither Karen nor I said anything. After all the crying that took place during the funeral, we were a bit shocked to hear our father's matter-of-fact statement. But I guess it was his way of closing the door on this part of our lives.

"Kids, I'm tired of Boston. I've lived there my whole life and I'm desperate for change. And that's why I'm moving in a few weeks. I've already placed the deposit on a house in Coral Gables and you're of course welcome to come and stay there anytime you want."

And that was that. My father was selling the house - cutting strings, cleaning up, and setting up shop elsewhere. He was moving on in his life and expected us to do it too.

So we did.

***

I call my father and tell him I'm coming for a visit, but not much more. Like I predicted, he doesn't ask why I want to visit him all of a sudden. The fact is I'm coming and he'll be happy to see me.

I also feel it's my obligation to text Gwen and write how much I appreciate all her help and that I'm going away a little while to see my father. She writes back in a few minutes, wishing me good luck and a healthy recovery. For some reason I had expected her to be more "in love" in her tone, but maybe I should be happy she's not planning on stalking me, which has happened with other girls in the past.

Before packing my bags, I also text my assistant Angela and tell her to cancel all my meetings for two weeks. I write that I'll be going away for personal reasons, which is the professional way to tell someone that something is wrong. I know I probably have a couple of very important meetings to attend, but Angela will deal with those. She can hand them over to Jim. They'll be fine - possibly even better - without me. I don't know if that's supposed to make me feel good, because it doesn't.

I book a trip to Miami online and throw some clothes in the black trolley bag I always use and call a cab. I'm getting out of here the fastest way possible.

I've never felt such an urgency to leave the city, my apartment, my job and my old life behind.

***

The plane trip to Miami is bumpy and my stomach is playing tricks on me. Turbulence usually don't unsettle me at all, being quite an experienced flyer, but today I'm really jumpy. For some reason I feel this might be the day where my luck with planes run out. My inner eye sees pictures of the plane crashing, my hands are sweating and my belly is making sounds of discontent. I'm something of a wreck myself, so I hope the plane at least remains intact. I'm wiping my hands on my pants' legs, a nervous tick I have, and when the plane abruptly jolts up and then sinks down, I feel something coming up my throat and I reach for a bag. But nothing happens and after a while the sickness subsides.

I'm dying for a drink or three.

I press a button and a plump, pasty pimple-scarred blonde stewardess with her eyes too far apart and a forced smile appears. I have a distinct feeling the general attractiveness of air hostesses has plummeted over the years. Aren't they supposed to look good? I want to follow a nice ass with my eyes down the aisle, not wonder why she doesn't use proper skincare products.

I'm also reminded that flying business class is no guarantee for a nice flight, despite the extra leg space. You have no control over turbulence, you don't get more attractive personnel and there's no guarantee against pesky seat neighbors either. The older fashionable lady with beaver-brown hair and giant oversized sunglasses is a good example. Her outfit is depressingly color-coded with purple and green as the theme. She wears really strong perfume which smells like over-sprayed odor-remover and has more gold jewelry than a flea market. Every now and then she produces loud smacks as she's sucking on some kind of hard candy or possibly a tooth she's about to lose.

Learning: business class is over-rated.

Finally we touch ground in Miami. It's a sticky September day and I'm happy I packed lightly. I actually feel a bit liberated to be somewhere else right now. New York lies very deep in my bones and it's still the greatest city in the world, but you need to get out of there sometimes not to let it swallow you.

I see my father as soon as I walk through the exit doors of Miami International Airport. He's standing next to his giant Toyota SUV, looking younger than I remember him. His skin is tan as always and his grey hair has some extra white from the last time I saw him, but otherwise it's quite clear - my father refuses to age. He told me once he enjoys life too much to let it run away from him and that's a quality I really admire.

My father's style of clothes is post-golf-round chic - he always looks like he came straight from the golf course. Today he's wearing a light-yellow Lacoste polo shirt and black chinos, and looks impressively neat and tidy except for some grass stains on his left leg.

He shines up when he sees me and gives me his custom bone-crushing hug, "Welcome son, such a long time!"

"Yeah, Christmas, right? Nice to see you, dad." I say, as I put my hand luggage in the back seat of his Toyota and admit to myself it really is nice to see him.

"Have you been golfing?" I nod towards his pants leg. My father's a very serious golf player, in fact so serious he's the director of the local golf course where he plays almost every day. I don't think he can do things less than very seriously.

"Yes, I have. I come directly from my best round in a long, long time - 82. Progress!"

My father beams. He's practically obsessed with improvement, in everything.

"82? I'm impressed!" I say before I climb into the car and we drive off.

"So how's life? I heard you're dating someone."

This makes my father smile in that silly way of people in love.

"Karen told you of course. Yes, I've met someone and it feels very good. She's absolutely gorgeous and I'm sure you'll like her. Her name is Melody."

Melody? Melody? Karen's right, it does sound like a pornstar name. But if my father hasn't picked up on this, I'm not going to make a fuss about it. Sometimes it's better to shut your mouth, something I'm just about starting to understand.

"Great, that's just great. So she's living with you now or what? I'm not going to be in the way or anything?"

"Yes, she is, and no, of course you're not going to be in the way! You're my son. Besides, she's just excited to finally meet you, after everything she's heard about you."

I haven't talked to my father in quite a while, so I'm happily surprised he's talked to this Melody about me. But I know he's proud, although he doesn't always say it.

"So, how have you been, son?" He says it casually, like he expects a normal, neutral or positive reply, and somehow I can't give him my real answer right now. Maybe later, when we get some more time to talk, but not now, not like this.

"I'm okay, just a lot to do at work. I really needed to get away, so I thought I'd come here and see how you're doing."

"Well that's just swell, son."

We sit silently for a while. My father's thinking about something, maybe his golf round, maybe his Melody, and I don't really know what to say, so I just watch the road feeling slightly lighter in my body. I'm happy to be here, in the car with him.

"Any women in your life right now?" I knew this question would show up sooner or later (it always does), but I still jump at it. My father's obsessed with the procreation of the Reynolds genes and neither my sister nor I give him anything to be happy about.

"Not really anything serious, no." I hate this topic and I think adult children all over the world do too. My dad, pretending not to hear my annoyance with the subject, soldiers on.

"I think it's about time you start getting serious. Why not settle down? You're a good-looking man, and I know you don't have any problems meeting women."

"Yeah, but I need to find the right woman first, right? Not just any nice one."

"Son, you can't wait around for Miss Perfect, because she doesn't exist. Everybody has problems and weaknesses. What you have to do is look past them and focus on the good things instead. If it feels good with someone then why not give her a real chance? You're not 20 anymore," says my father, who's 60 years old and dating a woman half his age.

Was coming here really a good idea? It took me about two minutes to change my mind, because I'm already annoyed with my father and his stubbornness. I'm reminded this kind of talk is exactly why I don't call him more often. He expects progress and I can't give him any, at least not when it comes to relationships or grandchildren. But I don't want to fight with him, feeling as fragile as I do right now, so I say, "Yes, I know, I know."

We're nearing Coral Gables, closing in on his house. The Gables is a nicely constructed garden city with many beautiful houses, tree-lined streets, historic architecture and quaint shops. I could've taken that from the local council website, I know, but it really is an almost idyllic city. At least most people thought so until September two years ago when they stabbed a child to death at a high school.

Things like this could happen anywhere it seems, so you might as well live in New York.

We reach the house and it looks bigger than I remember it - white, massive, luxurious - not a bachelor's place, but a bachelor's palace.

I came here with Karen just after he'd bought it, we drank a few beers by the pool, drove around the Gables, told dad he was right to move here (that's what he wanted to hear) and then unsentimentally went back to New York. Both Karen and I are New Yorkers and have a hard time seeing ourselves living anywhere else, but my father's Gables home is perfect for him as it's near the river, there's space for a boat (he can have breakfast in the kitchen while looking at it, thanks to roof-to-ceiling windows), everything's modern and as a nice bonus there's a good-sized swimming pool and a patio that's great for barbecues and entertaining. It's quite a place for a 60-year-old bachelor.

Well, he's not really a bachelor anymore, which I'm reminded of as soon as we drive onto the driveway. There, as we park next to my father's second car - the beautiful silver Porsche 911 Carrera he treated himself to for his 60th birthday - is the famous Melody.

My first impression of Melody is that she's a typical American platinum blonde with a nice and natural smile, but a not so natural (but terrific!) body, which is easy to spot in a white top and skin-tight jeans. What strikes me the most is how short she is. Not like a midget or something, but she's at least a head shorter than me. She also looks really young and it feels awkward to see my old father bend down and plant a kiss on her cheek.

"Hi hunny," he says and then looks at me, "this is my son, Jack."

The blonde bombshell and I shake hands.

"Welcome to the Gables," she says and flashes me a blinding smile. I feel my father's hand on my back.

"Let me show you where you can place your stuff and we'll grab a beer out by the pool." We walk through the house and to the guest room, which looks exactly the same as last time I was here. It's a bit like a hotel – sparsely decorated, but nice and homely. I place my luggage on the bed and go out to the kitchen, where my father's already standing with two ice-cold Coronas. He hands me one and we walk out to a couple of sun-deck chairs overlooking the pool. Melody soon joins us, holding a glass of white wine. She's put on a sweater to protect herself from the afternoon chill, but she's attractive even in less boob-flashing wear. I give her a thorough look again and wonder what a woman like her could see in a 60-year-old man. Father figure? Money? Experience? Or is it just the perfect tan?

"So how's life in the Big Apple?" My father looks at me like he's sizing me up. He's probably starting to wonder what really brought me here. He knows as well as I do it's not Reynolds' style to go on spontaneous family trips, so he should sense something isn't quite right.

I'm not sure he likes to know about it though.

"Busy as always. Lots of things going on right now. We've got some problems with one of our biggest clients, which takes a lot of my time, but I'm sure we'll sort it out. It's just nice to get a break from it all." This is true, but only a tiny part of the story of course.

He acknowledges the information with a slight nod accompanied by a long sip of Corona. It's getting darker and the sun is setting in the background, painting the sky a dreamy mix of pink and orange.

My eyes travel to Melody again and she takes the look as a cue to enter the conversation. She asks about my flight and I tell her about the sneezing Prada lady, describing her as vividly as I can, which nets some laughter. I can be quite funny when I'm in the mood and there's a beautiful woman to impress.

"Jack always had a way with words." My father says and I'm almost sensing some rivalry in his voice. Here's a woman who's young and beautiful enough to be my girlfriend and he knows it.

Dad tells me about some of the work he's done on the house, none of which I really register. I keep looking over at Melody instead. It's probably an inappropriate amount of looking considering she's my father's girlfriend, but I can't help it. My eyes are drawn to her perky fake breasts, her bleached smile, and her peroxide hair. Dad doesn't seem to notice and instead goes on about his boat, the house and the golf club. He asks me about Karen, wondering if she's really happy (he of course disapproves of Dylan as much as I do) and I tell him as much as I know, she seems happy in her own Karen-like way. He finishes his beer and gives me a pat on the shoulder. "Another one?" Then he goes out into the kitchen while I turn to Melody.

One question has been burning in my mind since I came here: "So how did you two meet?" Because I can bet my left butt cheek it wasn't on the golf course.

"At a club," Melody says matter-of-factly. "I used to be a dancer and Hank used to come there and tip me an awful lot [laughs]. I noticed there was something very special about him."

Was this before or after he put money in your panties? I feel like asking, but don't.

"Then one night he asked me if I wanted to go out for a drink and now, a few months later, I'm here." Melody shrugs like it was the most natural thing in the world for a 60-year-old man to pick up a girl half his age in a nightclub and start a relationship with her.

"A dancer? You mean like a stripper?" Is my father going to strip clubs? I wish I was surprised, but for some reason I'm not.

Melody laughs. "Yeah, if that's what you want to call it. We who work in the business like to call it exotic dancer. Sounds a bit more respectful."

It sure sounds exotic to be dating a stripper. My father obviously has some tricks up his sleeve I didn't know about.

"Wow, that's some story. So you still dance?"

"Nah, Hank thought I'd better quit and move in with him. I couldn't really say no to that. I actually really want to be an actress or something, I just started dancing because it's easy money."

Of course, they all want to be actresses. But I'm curious about these stereotypes, especially the attractive ones, and that's why I venture in the land of pick-up clichés.

"So have you ever done any modeling?" I say this in a casual way to acknowledge I find her attractive, a need I have with all beautiful women and a passive form of flirting I've learned to master. The good thing about it is you don't commit to anything, because objectively you're just being nice.

Melody giggles and says she never has. To be honest, I don't think they want models who are that short, at least not in the fashion industry, but a sleazy men's mag spread wouldn't surprise me at all. I casually throw in a "why not?" as it would be a good career choice considering her aspirations to become an actress. I'm again implying I think she's beautiful, not considering I might be treading on some flimsy moral ground here.

I abruptly abort the mission of passively hitting on Melody (I at least avert my interested gaze) because here comes her boyfriend/my father with a nicely put-together platter of grapes, crackers, sausages, and different kinds of cheese.

"You know what?" he says, as he puts the wooden tray down on the table, "why don't you come with us to the yacht club party tomorrow, maybe you can meet someone there, huh? End that single life of yours, settle down in the Gables and become my golf buddy." He chuckles loudly, but I'm not sure if he's joking or not.

"Ha-ha, maybe when I'm 60, pops. Besides, I love New York too much, couldn't live anywhere else."

"I would looove to go to New York. Can you believe I've never been? It seems like such an amazing place." Melody lights up like a kid. Compared to my father, she is of course.

"You've never been to New York? It's the greatest city in the world, I'm telling you. You must come and visit."

Dad wants to include himself in the New York plan, possibly sensing Melody and I have hit it off a little too well.

"Of course we should go to New York, Mel. We can come and visit you, Jack. Just tell me when you'll have us and we'll be there."

I don't like having people living at my place, never have and never will, but I say "yes, any time,". Then I tell them I will tag along to the yacht party, because what harm can it do to spend some more time with the beautiful Melody?

In the background of the friendly beer drinking and platter-snacking there's a soul-draining tiredness in me I haven't felt or at least noticed before. It feels like I need to sleep for days, weeks, maybe years to catch up. So I tell the two unlikely lovebirds it's time for me to hit the hay. My father, who can't seem to keep his hands off of his young girlfriend, asks me if I want to join his early morning golf round tomorrow, but I tell him I need my sleep.

"I guess Melody could take you around the Gables instead, show you the city. You're going shopping tomorrow, right Mel? Do you mind taking Jack around a bit?"

My heart leaps. I'm a bit surprised my father's insisting on his young and hot girlfriend taking me out for a Gables tour, but then maybe he doesn't realize how weak I am around women.

Melody is all smiles.

"No, not at all. If you don't mind shopping with a woman?" She gives me a quirky look and I'm starting to think she's flirting with me too.

"Ha-ha, no, that's fine. It will be fun." For me, everything involving pretty women is classified as "fun".

Then we end up having one more beer before we call it a night. As I'm sitting there watching my father and Melody snuggle, I admit feeling like the fifth wheel and extreme pangs of jealousy follow me to the bedroom and stay with me during the night.

I simply can't stop thinking about her.

***

I sleep and dream that my father (who in my dream is three feet taller than in real life) is chasing me around Manhattan with a shovel screaming: "you're a disappointment, Jack, you're such a fucking disappointment." I wake up at ten, damp from my own sweat and dry as a desert. I have a light headache, probably from the dehydration and although I got ten hours of sleep, I'm exhausted. I crawl out of bed and stretch my back with a crack and stumble to the window of the guest room, open the blinds and find another sunny day in the Gables. My spirits lift slightly, but are soon put down again by me wondering why someone from work hasn't even tried to call me yet. People rarely respect vacations or even sick leave like this one - they call anyway. They need something and they're mostly too lazy to look for it themselves. Maybe Angela has found a way to fend off all the calls? Strangely, instead of it making me feel relaxed, it leaves me feeling hollow, unwanted. My chest is tightening again and I need to breathe. In and out, in and out. Just like Gwen told me, it's all in the breathing.

I sit down on the bed again. I need to think of something else and badly and somehow my thoughts find Melody and her oversized breasts, her cute little body, her killer smile and it works - the blood shifts heads and so I shower and jerk off the negative thoughts. Instead I try to keep my head focused on the day ahead, the shopping with Melody and the yacht party. Because this can be a very pleasant day if I don't let myself destroy it.

***

It's shorts weather, but I hate shorts. They're geeky and unmanly and there's nothing attractive in a pair of hairy man-legs. Besides, despite Melody being my father's girlfriend and definitely off-limits to me, I want her to think I'm handsome and no one's handsome in shorts. So I wear jeans and put on a white Armani shirt, some semi-aggressive cologne and comb my dark hair backwards. I look like a casual stockbroker ready to brag about my new yacht and my gold-blue Rolex adds to the classy touch. It's a good look.

In the kitchen I find Melody sipping her morning coffee and skimming through a gossip magazine. She looks amazingly tan and alive in a light-yellow summer dress.

"Good morning," she says. "Did you sleep well?"

"Morning, Mel." Is it too early to call her Mel? Well, it's in any way better than Melody.

"I slept like a baby, thank you very much. Is there any coffee there for me?"

Melody takes out a cup that says "World's best dad", which I remember buying for my father when I was 12 or something (an uncharacteristic emotional expression for our family), and pours me a cup.

"Let's head outside," she says and we sit down by the table where we had our beers last night. It's already hot and I'm happy to be in a spot with some shade.

We quietly sip our coffee and just when it's about to get a bit awkward, I break the silence by asking her what she's shopping for. "Clothes mostly," she says, which I don't know if I should take as a joke or not - I didn't think she was going to buy a toaster. But Melody seems to have that straightforward, literal way which is quite refreshing for a guy who works in a business where sarcasm is your bread and butter. So I try to keep my usually mean jokes to a minimum and focus on being charming "Hank Junior".

We smalltalk and I get the feeling there's definitely some kind of chemistry between us. I'm even beginning to wonder where we're heading with this. But some casual flirting can't do any harm right? We're both adults here - we know the rules.

I must admit though that I was never any good at sticking to them.

***

We hit the road in my father's silver Porsche 911. Melody's at the wheel and she's driving like she doesn't intend to do anything afterwards, ever. I was tired, but now I'm wide-awake, trying to figure out whether I'm going to die or not. It's a miracle we get from point A to B without injuries. Point B is in this case a parking lot outside a big shopping mall in the Gables. When Melody finally turns off the engine I manage to say:

"Wow, you training to be a race car driver or something?" I let out a nervous laugh, which I hope doesn't upset my manly image.

"Ha-ha, I just like driving fast, always have. Gives me a huge kick."

"Good for you. I was never much interested in either cars or driving to be honest." I wasn't. Not my thing. And in New York you don't really need to be either.

"So what do you like to do, Jack?"

"I don't have many hobbies to be honest, don't have time for them. I used to read a lot, but when I get home from work I'm often too tired. I do enjoy a walk through Central Park or a dinner with friends." I avoid mentioning one of the things I take most pleasure out of doing, is women.

"Hope you don't take this the wrong way, but that sounds pretty boring to me. All that work - don't you ever get sick of it?"

"Well, not until recently I didn't. I like my job - it's challenging and creative. I guess it's a bit of a cliché but I'm an entrepreneur at heart. I remember how I used to sell stuff when I was a kid, freshly squeezed orange juice, I created a neighborhood newspaper, I cut people's lawns - anything I could come up with. Probably got it from my father."

Melody smiles. "Yeah, I could see that. You're both very alike, except for the hobbies thing maybe. Hank always has something planned, tennis lessons, the daily golf round, scuba diving or boat trips. There's always something happening around him, I like that."

"Yeah, he's young for his age."

This is maybe a cheap stab at their age difference, but I can't really get used to the fact that Melody is half, yes half, the age of my father. But I guess if it doesn't disturb her, then I shouldn't let it disturb me. But it does.

I never really liked shopping and shopping with Melody doesn't change that view. She just wanders around aimlessly between the different stores and seems to look at everything and nothing. When I shop I need a clear purpose, a list, some direction, otherwise I'd never even enter a store. But this is a woman's thing I suppose.

After a while she actually decides to try on a few dresses. I stand outside the stall like a boyfriend and Melody asks me about my opinion for every single item (I'm just sad she doesn't try on underwear), and I basically give a tired thumbs up for everything (although there's a pink skirt which I think looks horrible - on anyone), which is honest in a way because Melody really looks fantastic, but also because I'm dead tired and hungry and want her to buy a few things and finish up so we can have lunch. But my encouragement of course makes her buy more and more and in the end I feel sorry for her credit cards since they must be as sore as my feet, being dragged forwards and backwards like that. I don't know if this is what she means by "showing me the Gables", because if I knew I would've sat down outside with a cup of coffee and waited, although I would've missed the show.

We finally sit down at an indoor garden-style Italian restaurant and I'm dying for a drink. I order a Skinny bitch (which may sound like a prostitute but is really just vodka and mineral water) and a glass of Sicilian Chardonnay for Melody.

"Poor you," she says, gently touching me on my shoulder, "you must be dead tired after all that running around."

"I'm fine," I say, slightly aroused by the touching. "I'm here to get away from work so it's good you keep my head occupied, although I admit my feet are a bit beaten up." I smile at her. It's an exhausted smile, but it's the best I can do.

"So this work thing, how bad is it?"

"I don't know. I didn't even know it was bad until very recently. When a doctor told me."

Melody takes a sip of wine and seems to ponder my answer.

"A doctor told you? That sounds serious. But I guess sometimes you need someone to tell you these things – hopefully not a doctor though. I know it's easy for me to say, since I'm not working right now, but work isn't life. You work to support life, right? Not the other way around." Melody's big eyes are waiting for an answer.

"Right, but the sad part is I don't seem to have a life besides work."

Ouch! Where did that come from? I surely did not just tell a woman I have no life?

Saying it out loud makes me realize how true it is though and it opens some kind of vent inside of me and I end up spilling the beans completely about my breakdown. Words are pouring out of my mouth so fast I barely have time to drink, while Melody's mostly quiet, looking a tiny bit uncomfortable, but definitely listening.

But when I start questioning my career motives she just blurts out, "Jack, I hear what you're saying and I understand you're questioning things, but I don't think you're entirely fair to yourself. Are you saying the years you put into your career are wasted? Haven't you fulfilled at least one of your dreams?"

She's right of course. I've accomplished a whole lot of things, basically every bullet point on my list of goals. It does account for something.

"I'm actually jealous of you, Jack. You've had an amazing career and not many people have achieved that kind of success. It's never too late to focus on other things if that's what you want."

"It doesn't sound so bad when you put it like that." I smile at her because she really makes me feel good. Question is: am I getting too comfortable around her?

"You haven't told Hank yet, have you? He doesn't know anything? From the way he talks he still seems to think your biggest problem is the lack of a woman in your life."

"Nah, we don't talk so much about these things, never did. I don't know if I want to tell him about it either, he never really liked hearing about weakness or problems."

"And yet you told me, Jack. I'm flattered." An intoxicating smile follows.

"I'm happy I did." We exchange smiles again and I'm starting to wonder if we've passed into the realm of serious flirting.

While we eat and drink, I decide to turn the tables a bit - I start asking the questions. I want to know more about her and what I learn is that Melody's a Boise girl with Mormon parents who doesn't talk to her after she fled both the faith and the city after high school and got into a far more funky lifestyle in Miami, working in bars, dancing, partying and compensating for a childhood which she describes as safe, but dull.

"So you ran from home?" I ask her.

"Yeah, you can say I ran - I ran as far away as I could. I just couldn't stand it out there and it was kind of my teenage rebellion. I had no idea what I wanted, I just didn't want to stay in Boise and turn into my mother. And that got me to Miami, without money, without knowing anyone. I met a girl named Julie, we became friends and shared a crummy old apartment. It was a struggle, just getting enough money to pay the rent was tough, but at least I got out from that hellhole." Melody sounds sad when she's telling the story, like it didn't exactly turn out the way she wanted it to.

"It was not exactly what my parents had in my mind. They love the snow and the quiet life, while I'm just the opposite. I wasn't an easy child for them - always goofing off, doing crazy things. All my frustration, my anger about my boring life, I took it out on them."

"It has taken them a long time to forgive me, to understand me, but now we're okay. Although I haven't even talked to them about Hank yet – I'm not sure how they would react to me seeing a 60-year-old man, and I don't want to risk disappointing them anymore. Luckily, I have a kid brother who's shouldering their lifestyle - he's already married with kids. At least they got half of them right."

I look at Melody who has been talking uninterrupted for a while. I see her more clearly now and it makes her even more beautiful than before. I decide to ask her what's been itching on my brain for a while:

"Your name isn't really Melody, right?"

Melody shines up like I just delivered some good news, "No, it isn't. How did you know?"

"It didn't seem like something two Mormons would name their child, that's all."

Melody chuckles, "Well, actually it is now. But I changed it. I was born Melanie, thought it very much out of character, so changed it. I definitely feel more like a Melody." She smiles at me like I'm the only one in on this "secret". Happy to get it out of the way, I continue my questioning.

"So are you really happy living here in the Gables, I mean you're still young and my father's friends...they're, they're quite old."

"Yes, I like it here, it's a nice contrast to Miami. Besides, if I want to party or get the nightlife vibe, I can always go to Miami for the day."

I can't shake the feeling it makes no sense for a girl like Melody to be dating a 60-year-old man – even if he's my father (well, especially since he's my father). But I don't say anything - I need to drink more to do that.

We talk and talk and talk some more and soon two and a half hours have passed. Melody looks down at her watch and makes a face. Dad's golf round was over a long time ago, there's a party tonight and no matter how good and natural this moment feels - it has to end.

I pay the bill and as we're heading back to the car, I glance over at her and think oh my god she's beautiful, but my eyes linger a little too long. Her eyes find mine and I know for sure - we're falling for each other.

I'm treading very dangerous water here. I really need to take a few steps back and abort the mission.

But how can I, when I want her so badly?

***

I always felt comfortable at parties. I love mingling, drinking, and connecting with strangers and friends, while at the same time being able to hide, leave whenever I feel like it, or carry on with my drink. If you're in a party or a nightclub, there's too much going on for people to notice you all the time, and so it becomes the best possible escape, from work, from yourself, from everything. The trick is of course to find that silver lining of drunkenness where you maximize your enjoyment without making a fool out of yourself. Sometimes I'm balancing on it and sometimes I trip over, and it's when I trip over that ugly Jack comes out, the Jack who lets his demons rule. That Jack can be quite a jack-ass, if you excuse the pun.

I'm going to do my best not to trip over the line tonight though and it shouldn't be too difficult, since The Coral Gables Yacht Club party isn't exactly up my alley. Old people roam the room like drunken alligators, touching shoulders, slapping backs, saying something half-funny and chuckling, just like rich, old people always do. They seem to be drinking like there's no tomorrow, because at their age, who knows if there will be?

My father's sprightly compared to many of these white-haired men and their Botox-infused wives who look like someone ironed all their wrinkles and possibility of facial expressions away. There's a strong odor - a mix of old man's sweat, old woman's cologne and sea breeze, which makes me reluctant to drink, although I'm sure it's exactly what I need to have a decent time. I have no idea how Melody could tag along to something like this, it's like stepping straight into the history channel. When I go out I want to feel young again, not talk pension plans.

My father's proudly parading Melody around the room, carefully explaining that the young blonde next to him is his girlfriend, because it's too easy to assume it's his daughter. I'm introduced as the son of course and everybody seems surprised I even exist, which I find both disappointing and awkward. I get a lot of overpowering handshakes from testosterone-heavy older men, but the only names I make out, are Burt and Tom. It's very confusing because they all look alike with their sun-red skin, white hair, bleached teeth and they all talk about boats like it's the greatest thing in the world to be on water. Many of them ask if I have a boat and I say no, never had one, never will, the reason being I don't trust water well enough. This of course makes me as misplaced at this party as a dog in a goldfish bowl.

While my dad is mingling with his comrades and kissing their wrinkle-free wives on their stretched cheeks, I whisper to Melody: "Have you really been to this kind of party before? How do you survive?"

"Ha-ha, are you bored already, Jack? The party is going to get better though. They just need to get more drunk and suddenly all hell will break loose. I've gone to similar events and witnessed people falling over, throwing snide comments at each other and if we're really lucky we might even catch a fight." Melody might be right about that, but I don't find much enjoyment in old people looking silly, especially not if they include my father, who I always respected.

"Well, I hope something more exciting's bound to happen soon, because I'm not very good at talking to these people. I mean, are there other topics than cars, boats and golf? And I don't want to talk about my father, because that will make me feel like 12 again."

"Don't worry, most of them are actually quite nice and you can get into a few interesting conversations once in a while if you stay away from their "it was better back then"-discussions. I'm going to the restroom, can you hold on to my drink?"

I take Melody's drink and watch her beautiful ass bounce away to the yacht club bathroom. Her evening dress is black, tasteful, short and inviting to fantasize about.

I don't like being left alone in this marine version of Jurassic Park - it makes me feel like a slab of fresh meat in an area full of velociraptors. I decide to try and stay away from awkward conversations and sit down in one of the sofas while I wait for Melody to return. But my hiding isn't very successful, because soon a fox-haired woman sits down next to me. She wears a ton of lipstick, an exceptionally tan face, an orange business suit, light-blue eye shadow and she seems pretty hammered.

"I haven't seen yoouuu around," she says, "are you a new member of the club?" She's looking straight at me, seeking eye contact, but having obvious trouble to focus her eyes.

"No, I'm here visiting my father," I say, pointing to my dad, now standing out on the terrace at the other end of the room, puffing on a big cigar and looking like he's having the time of his life.

"Ahh," she says, "I knoooow Hank! So you're his son, how nice to meet you!" The woman gives me a hug and almost suffocates me with her perfume. It's like putting a knife up my nostril.

"Nice meeting you too." I say, trying to smile as genuine a fake smile as possible.

"I'm Felicity," she says pointing to herself like she's talking to a retard.

"Jack," I reply.

"So what do you think of the Gables?"

"It's nice, perfect really if you like golf and boats (and is a hundred years old). My father loves it here - myself I'm more of a New Yorker."

"New York is nice." Felicity says like she has to. I should obviously have been more generous with my remarks about the Gables. "But don't you find there are too many people there, too much stress, too much violence?" The orange dragon continues with a slight slur.

"Nah, New York is the perfect city to me, it has it all. And it's not really that violent." I'm so bored I'm thinking of starting a city war with this Felicity. Maybe it will spice this party up or at least make her leave me alone. But Felicity's of course undeterred in her drunken enthusiasm.

"In the Gables I think we have the really perfect city, being close to Miami if you want the nightlife, but still quiet with ample shopping opportunities (did she just say ample?), lots of things to do and very friendly people. We're also doing many things to improve. Right now we're working on a project..."

Luckily, Melody arrives and saves me. I excuse myself from Felicity's grasp right before she's about to get into landscaping details or five-year community plans and head outside, leaving a slightly surprised and annoyed orange lady behind.

"Thanks," I say and lift my glass to Melody, "thanks for saving me."

"Well, I understood you were in trouble when I saw Felicity's orange warning dress. She's famous for talking people to death. She attacked me the first time

I was here and if you try to be nice with her she'll just go on, and on, and on." Melody makes a talking gesture with her hand.

I chuckle, "Yeah, I saw it coming."

We walk away from the party in the clubhouse and out on the pier by the boats.

"I must tell you something about the Gables," I say, "although it's packed with old people, it's pretty nice."

"So Felicity got through to you?" Melody says with a cute smirk on her face and then continues, "no, but you're right, it's nice here. Although New York sounds pretty cool too."

"Yeah, New York is...it's New York."

We walk out among the boats, the air is gentle, the lights are bathing in the water and the alcohol is doing its little thing, easing my tense head. Soon we're so far away we can't see the yacht club.

"Time to head back maybe?" I say, and turn around to find Melody looking at me. Her green eyes are asking a question I'm not properly prepared for. She's so close to me I could bend down and kiss her and that's exactly what I do, almost like reflex. Her lips welcome mine and I put my hand on her lower back.

We kiss for a long time and my blood's starting to boil when suddenly Melody pulls away from me. She's in shock.

"I can't believe we just did that, I don't know what came over me!"

I don't know what to say really, I know what came over me and I know we both wanted it. But I also know it's wrong, so wrong, and I need to start thinking with the right head again. So I say in a hopefully reassuring voice:

"Melody, it's just a kiss. We're both a bit drunk and we lost it for a bit. It doesn't mean anything. Don't worry about it. These things happen."

I don't know who I'm trying to convince with this cascade of clichés. We're not really drunk and this didn't happen by accident, we both know that.

"But I feel horrible, really horrible. I can't believe I betrayed Hank like that."

"Don't worry about it Mel, it's one friendly kiss. One kiss."

Melody's wiping the tears from her eyes with her knuckle. "Was that a friendly kiss to you? Is that how you kiss your friends?"

"Like I said, it was a one-time thing. We gave in to the moment." I know I ought to stop talking like this, as there's no point to it, but I'm trying to soothe myself more than Melody right now.

"It's not only the kiss, Jack, I'm really attracted to you. I know I shouldn't be, but I am."

Melody looks at me like a puppy and I want to take her into my arms and kiss her again, but for once my conscience speaks up and tells me it's not the right thing to do. I never wanted to go behind my father's back of course, but I've crossed the line by a mile now and I need to retreat. And I need to cover up my tracks.

"Melody, I don't know what to say. I like you too - you're great. But we just can't...you know. So let's forget this kiss ever happened, okay? You can do that right?"

Disappointment drapes Melody's face, "but...?"

Oh crap, what have I gotten myself into?

***

I wake up at five in the morning with a headache and a damp shirt. I'm not hung-over in the alcoholic sense - the hangover I have is rather related to me making out (yeah, it wasn't just a kiss) with my father's girlfriend. Do I regret it? You bet! I shouldn't have started hitting on her in the first place! What kind of person does that? Am I so sick and twisted and lonely, I can't even leave my poor father alone? I came here to get his help to solve my problems, not create new ones. Now the only thing Melody and I can do is shut our mouths and pretend like these feelings don't exist and that kiss never happened.

But I don't really know how good Melody's acting skills are and her seemingly very emotional nature worries me. Wanting to be an actress and actually being a good one, are two very different things. What happens if she tells my father?

I don't get any further in my negative spiral of thoughts because I see my phone vibrating on the bed stand. Who calls at this time in the morning? Mike? He must be drunk.

"Hi Mike, what's up?"

"I'm breaking up with Jo," Mike says. But it doesn't sound like Mike - this person is so angry his voice is shaking. "That bitch cheated on me! Can you believe that? Fuck! Can I come over?"

"What? What did you just say?" All my thoughts about my current situation are wiped away - here's some completely new shit brought to light.

"It's over. I'm breaking up with Jo. I found messages, cheating fucking messages. She admitted to it all and didn't even flinch! That bitch! Where are you?"

"Ehhmmm, I'm visiting my father in the Gables, you know, outside Miami?"

"What? You're in Miami? Why haven't you told me?"

"Coral Gables to be exact, it's close to Miami. I'm sorry man, it was a spur-of-the-moment kind of thing. Long story. I can tell you when I get back."

"When is that?" Mike's impatient for my brotherly understanding.

"Don't know, a few more days, maybe a week."

"Fuck that, I'm coming there."

"What?" This is surely not Mike talking.

And he's not talking anymore, because he's hung up on me. When I try to call him back, he doesn't pick up, so I try again, but nothing. Maybe he's passed out or maybe's he's really on his way to the airport.

I'm so confused right now I feel dizzy. What's going on? Why is everybody hanging up one me? Why did I kiss my father's girlfriend?

It's five in the morning and I'm exhausted, but it takes me at least an hour of tossing and turning before I manage to find the well-needed state of sleep.

***

The next time I look at the clock it says 10:30. Yowza! I slept long. I shower, dress and get down to the kitchen, happy to find the house is still silent. My father was in a pretty rough shape yesterday, so he'll need his sleep. I desperately need a cup of coffee myself, but don't want to turn on the espresso machine and wake the whole house (the old-school machine sounds like a meat grinder), so instead I go for my father's favorite instant coffee and turn on the electric kettle.

The first clear thought I have is that I have to stop thinking with my dick, as it always points me into trouble. What my father said about progress never really got into that egotistic lower head of mine. I grab my cup of coffee and walk out on the patio, past the pool and down to the bridge where my father keeps his boat. The water is sparkling, the sun playing on it, making it look like a disco ball. I wish I could just dive in there and clean myself from trouble, from everything - turn back the clock and rise from the water as a born-again. But I know I can't. We all need to face our consequences.

A few minutes later, I hear a voice from behind.

"Nice day, huh?" It's Melody and she doesn't sound very confident.

I'm definitely not ready for this kind of confrontation yet, but I reply: "Yeah, beautiful," and tilt my head back and look at her. She looks like she's been crying.

"Dad still asleep?"

"Yeah, he had a rough one last night. I mean he sure had fun, but he'll need some aspirins today that's for sure." A nervous giggle. "What about you?"

"Nah, I'm fine, I didn't drink that much."

We're feeling each other out, talking about everything except the MISTAKE.

"You want to go somewhere? Have breakfast? Talk?"

Melody's voice is weak and she looks down on her feet. She's as lost as I am, but at least she's not dodging the bullet like I usually do in these situations.

Not that I'm used to making out with my father's girlfriend.

"Yeah, sure. I'll drive though." I flash her a smile.

I finish my coffee and put it by the kitchen sink while Melody writes a note to my sleeping dad. Then we head over to the Porsche. I feel uneasy, like we're teenagers on the run, but at this moment I've got no better idea than to talk it out. I reverse out from the driveway and turn to Melody.

"Where to?"

"Take a left and just drive, please. I know a place."

I drive on. We hardly say anything. To say there's tension here is to say the sea is blue.

"Go right here," Melody says, after we've been driving in silence for close to 20 minutes. She's pointing towards a dirt road, leading, as it looks, into some kind of field.

"You sure?"

She nods.

We pass some empty houses, overgrown lawns, and a lonely wooden chair. I'm starting to worry Melody's taking me to this abandoned place just to shoot me and do away with the body. It would be a fitting end to the story.

I'm sad I have to take the beautiful Porsche on a road this bad, but it doesn't take long before we reach the water. It's like a tiny little beach in the middle of nowhere. The grass around it is overgrown and not looked-after, but the place is still beautiful in a quiet and unexpected way. As soon as I see it, I understand why Melody wanted me to come here.

"Wow."

"It's nice, huh? I found this place a while ago and I have come back to it a few times since. I often go here myself because it's so quiet you can hear your own thoughts properly. It always calms me down and since I know how stressed you've been I wanted to show it to you."

Melody gives me a shy smile. I'm surprised and actually honored she wants me to see something so personal.

"You see those two trees over there," Melody says and points her index finger, "the ones that kind of bend in towards each other? I know it might sound corny but I actually think they are two old souls, two people. You see how the shape in between them kind of resembles a heart? I don't think that's a coincidence. This place has a very strong energy and if I'm down, it always gets me up somehow. I don't know if you believe in these things, but I think you do, otherwise I wouldn't have brought you here."

I look at the trees and think I really want to believe in these things. I'm not a religious man, not in the organized sense of the word, but I can really appreciate the beauty and spiritual power of nature. That's probably why I'm so attached to Central Park and know almost every tree in it. I never thought of myself like that, but maybe my affection for the green is my soft spot and it actually feels good to have one. I look over at Melody and find her looking straight back at me. A strong sense of heat overcomes me and all I want to do right now is to hold her and kiss her and make love to her. Throughout my life, this is the feeling I've never been able to resist - the power of a beautiful woman and the rush of that magic moment when you realize you want each other.

I reach out and place my hand on her thigh. We don't look at each other, but we feel it – the shivering heat. I'm helpless against it and I know I'm losing the battle against myself again. It might be the energy of the place or our combined weaknesses, but soon we're riding the waves of passion, giving in to them completely. We're releasing the tension we created by delving deeper into each other, kissing, touching and finally, (completing the treason) making love. It's the moment acting, the world letting loose completely - our thoughts, doubts, and consequences left aside.

But they will be preying on us as soon as it ends. We both know that.

***

The drive home is a guilt ride. I want to touch her, talk to her, console her, because she's crying now, but I'm not sure she would want to and that it would help. I'm completely confused about everything and I've never felt this guilty about sex before. I've fallen for a woman I, for practical and humanitarian reasons, can't possibly fall in love with, and together we have silently ripped my father's heart out. This is as wrong as it gets from every angle.

"Why did we do this? How could we? What are we going to do?" Melody says between tears. She's panicking now and I don't blame her. I have no solution up my sleeve, real nor imagined, so I don't say anything. Because what is there to say? All I know is I must get out of the Gables, because this is no longer a disaster waiting to happen, it's just a disaster.

My phone wakes me up again from the guilt stream. It's a message from Mike. In the hazy fumes of love I've completely forgotten about him and now I'm informed his plane is landing in less than an hour. I need to think fast.

"Mel, I know this may sound crazy, but I need to go to the airport. Can you take the car home from there?"

"What? Why do you need to go to the airport?"

"I completely forgot my friend Mike's coming to visit today! I put my palm against my forehead to illustrate my stupidity. I need to pick him up."

Melody looks confused, but she's hurting too much right now to say anything but: "Okay, yeah, I guess."

I feel sorry for her. This is my fault, I pushed her into this and now I'm running away. Because as we drive towards the airport, I know I'm not going back to my father's house. There's no way I can look him in the eye again, perhaps ever. I have everything I need to leave - the passport in my pants pocket and my wallet. No change of clothes or toothbrush of course, as they're still in my father's house, but that's a small problem in relation to everything else.

"Should I wait for you?" Melody says, as we park outside the terminal. She has no clue of what my plans are, poor thing.

"No, we'll probably have lunch first, just us guys. We have a lot of catching up to do. And I think it's best if you go back before Hank starts worrying about you. Tell him I'll be in later. We'll take a cab."

I kiss Melody on the cheek. It's a Judas kiss, a salty taste of betrayal. I'm distancing myself now, fading out, running away. It's not easy, but I've become an expert over the years.

I can see tears gently running down her cheek as she's driving away, but I can't let them get to me. I don't need them right now - I already have too much guilt inside. So I just wave to her, my heart burning down in my stomach.

***

I buy a Snickers bar while I wait for the plane from New York and eat it not with enjoyment, but with raw hunger and desperation. I'm feeling my chest tighten again and I put all my efforts on breathing in and breathing out, while shoveling the chocolate down.

I try to read the Miami Herald while I wait, but the words won't stick to my brain. I'm feeling sick, like the Gwen-date collapse all over again. I half-run to the bathroom, lean over one of the sinks and try to vomit, but nothing comes out. I stare at my face in the bathroom mirror and I don't know if I should feel hate or just sorry for myself. I guess a mix of both will do.

As I exit the bathroom, I see Mike standing fifty meters away, holding an aluminum carry-on luggage, looking absolutely lost, his head turning left and right like he's watching a tennis match. His eyes are red and a tuft of hair is standing up on the back of his head. He's wearing a plain and wrinkled black t-shirt, something I never thought he'd wear outside the comfort of his own bed. This is obviously not the best time in his life - in our lives.

Then he sees me and - without much of a facial expression - walks up to me and gives me a brotherly hug.

"You look like you've seen a ghost," he says.

"You look like you've slept with one," I counter.

"Mike, I know you're feeling shitty, you've just been on a flight and you want to sit down for a while, but we can't stay in Miami. We just can't and I'll tell you why in a minute. We're going," I scan the departures board above Mike's head, "to Cancun."

"Cancun? What? Why?"

"I will tell you on the plane, first we need tickets. Follow me."

I head over to the counter and manage to buy two last minute tickets to Cancun, Mexico. Mike just stands next to me, watching the show, too shocked and tired to keep asking me why I'm doing this and if it's a joke.

"But you have no luggage!" he says, as we walk briskly towards the gate.

I look at my friend's innocent face and say: "Believe me when I say it's the least of my problems."

***

After we sit down in our first class seats, Mike leans over and whispers, "Now, do you mind telling me what the fuck this is about?"

I look him straight in the eye and say in my normal, but serious voice:

"I slept with my father's girlfriend." Then I slowly repeat, "I slept with my father's girlfriend."

"You slept with your father's girlfriend?"

Mike's trying to taste the sentence in his mouth to see if it makes any sense. It doesn't.

"Yes, sadly and regretfully, I did. Now let me explain. My father has met this fantastic hot young girl named Melody, she's a bombshell - big fake tits, tight body, beautiful smile, all that. And she has great personality as well. So..."

I outline the events to Mike, after which he just stares at me.

"You're joking, right? This is too sick to be true, even by your standards."

"No, that's the true, but slightly abbreviated, version of what actually happened. I came here to see my father, to try to connect with him and talk to him about some stuff I've been thinking about lately, and instead of doing anything like that, I rip his heart out of his chest and stomp on it. I mean, how sick am I? They should put me behind bars."

"So he knows?"

"No, of course not, not unless Melody has told him. But I don't think she'd do that, I mean why would she do that?"

"I don't know. I don't know this Melody and neither do you, judging from your little story. What I'm wondering is how you're going to explain running away like this? Or are you just never going to talk to him again?"

Mike's always levelheaded and thinks of the things I don't even consider myself. This is of course one of those.

"I don't know. I'll figure something out, I just couldn't stand to look him in the eye."

During the plane trip I also tell Mike about my panic attack, my unlikely second date with Gwen, my time off work and my frequent thinking about my mother's death, our family, my father, Clara, my sister – things I never ever thought about before. Mike in turn tells me about finding sexually explicit text messages to and from an "R" in Joanne's phone. He tells me he approached her about it, hoping it was all a big joke, but ended up completely heartbroken when Joanne flat out admitted to cheating on him.

"It was like she didn't even care enough to lie," Mike says in disbelief.

After their talk Mike threw her out of the apartment in the middle of the night, drank a bottle of whisky and called me. And now here he is, next to me on a plane to Cancun, trying to cure a hangover from hell.

"I can't believe how she could do this to me."

I don't know how many times I've told Mike I have a bad feeling about Joanne. But I guess it would do him no good to remind him, so instead I try to get into my friendly Dr. Phil-mode again.

"I know it sounds stupid, but you've got to see this from the bright side, at least you've found out and can move on with your life. Who knows how long things like this can go on? Now you have the time to start afresh, find a better woman and enjoy a happier life."

"It's kind of hard to see it from the bright side when you love someone and they stab you in the back, Jack. Although I feel like killing her right now, I still love her and I'm not exactly ready to move on."

I must admit I don't understand the kind of love Mike has for Joanne, but that's probably because I never felt anything like it myself.

***

I still feel like shit when we enter the taxi that's supposed to take us to the hotel. The air is hot and sticky and a drop of sweat slides down my back, while a storm of guilt keeps swirling around in my head. I look over at Mike who has the appearance of an apnea victim ready to fall over. We're one good-looking duo.

The taxi driver makes it a trio and adds an eye-watering garlic smell to the equation. He's badly overweight, breathes heavily, sweats like a pig and displays two large circles under his armpits while he lifts Mike's bag into the trunk of the rundown old Mercedes. Like all taxi drivers in southbound tourist destinations, he drives like a complete lunatic, but my ride with Melody has prepared me for it and I can focus on shutting up my own guilt-ridden brain. Mike's mostly silent, probably thinking about his new life as a single man. He never liked being single, of course.

"Mike, what am I going to do about this?" I say in my whiniest voice possible. "You think I should just come clean, don't you?" Mike was always one in favor of the truth, whereas I'm not sure people can handle the truth, at least a truth as nasty as this one.

"I have no idea. Sounds like you should talk to Melody first and come up with a strategy."

"Yeah, but I guess I need to explain why I had to leave. What do I say?"

"Tell him an urgent business meeting came up and you had to take the first plane out of the Gables. With your work schedule it wouldn't be so far-fetched I guess, at least less incredible than the truth."

Mike continues his analysis:

"Your main worry here should be Melody cracking under the pressure and admitting everything. If I were you, I'd call her and discuss this."

"Mhm. Yeah, I guess. Fuck. I can't believe this...this mess."

"I don't know what to say, Jack, I feel pretty shitty myself. You know, I still see it like it's my fault in a way, that I pushed her to this." Catholic altar boy Mike lingers in the guilty mind frame, despite being completely innocent.

"Come on, Mike, you know that isn't true. You were the best boyfriend you could be. She should be thanking her lucky star for hooking up with you, because you treated her like a queen. You know that, I know that, fucking everybody knows that."

"I really ought to go back to New York and break that guy's nose." Mike spits out the words, splattering on the window.

I'm surprised and irritated by all this wrongly directed aggression. The one he should be angry with is Joanne.

"Is that really what you want to do, punch a guy in the face for saving you from Joanne? You should send him a thank-you-card, not punch him."

"But I love her, Jack. I love her! And just because you never liked her doesn't mean I'm suddenly happy she decided to sleep with someone else and end our relationship. It doesn't change the way I feel."

"So you love a person who cheats on you and treats you like shit?"

The cab driver throws us a look in the rear-view mirror. His English is poor, but good enough to sense that this is no friendly talk anymore.

"You don't seem to understand the concept of love, Jack. Did you ever really love anyone but yourself?"

Suddenly Mike's throwing everything at me but the kitchen sink. My reflex response would be to retaliate, but I'm too tired for that now. I realize I shouldn't have started this conversation in the first place, since it's obvious Jo still has her fangs deep into Mike's heart.

"Mike, I'm sorry, I'm full of shit as usual. Let's stop this nonsense - we're on vacation for God sakes."

I give Mike an innocent smile to show him I mean well and I don't want to argue with what could very well be the only close friend I have. We spend the rest of the ride in silence and I think about what Mike said, about me not understanding the concept of love. Is he right? Am I too self-centered to feel real love? It wouldn't surprise me, being a Reynolds and all. Maybe that's why I'm still single? I always thought my problem was my search for the love people make movies and write songs about, a Romeo and Juliet-kind of love - but maybe it's a bit of both. Women come easy to me, always have, but they leave me easily too, and they leave without leaving anything, if you know what I mean. No imprint on my heart, nothing. And that's why I let them go. It's not that I'm happy to be alone, I just haven't found another way to be.

Yet.

And in the turbulence of these troubling thoughts, we're there.

***

Mike looks pretty excited as we step out of the car and look around, like the taxi ride made him happier somehow. Maybe he's decided to at least try and have a good time on this strange impromptu trip. A gentle breeze from the ocean touches us.

"This was maybe not such a bad idea," he says, in a way forgiving me for the remarks I made about Joanne and also kind of forgetting what he said about me being unable to understand love.

"Sometimes I'm right, Mike. Although I won't blame you for thinking otherwise." I say with a smirk on my face. We tip the smelly cab driver and head inside. I'm again reminded I don't carry luggage. Something I would desperately need right now, because I smell too.

The hotel is the typical marble-infested five-star resort hotel with panoramic windows overlooking the sea. I didn't expect anything less or anything more, and I'm happy I saw the poster at the airport. Now all I need to find is an empty room.

There's a tiny woman with a mole next to her nose at the gigantic check-in desk. She's so small that if she were any shorter, I probably wouldn't see her. I give her a confident smile.

"Hi," I say.

"Welcome to Fiesta Americana Cancun, do you have a reservation?" She squeaks like a bird, her voice sounding like she inhaled an unhealthy dose of helium and squeezed her vocal chords together at the same time. I do my best not to look at Mike, because I know we would burst out laughing.

I compose myself, "No, I don't, are there any rooms free?"

The little bird looks at me suspiciously and starts hammering on her computer. She doesn't seem very optimistic and I'm starting to get nervous that we have to start chasing around for hotels, which would be a real letdown at this stage.

"It's quite busy, sir. All standard rooms are taken. We have two suites available though."

Since money is about the only thing I have, I tell her to put us in a suite, the bigger the better. I hand her my platinum credit card. I usually feel good doing that, showing off my wealth, but that buzz is long gone.

"Oh my God..." Mike says when we enter the Presidential suite, our home for the coming days. It's fantastic, with a beautiful sea-view terrace, separate bedrooms, and a big living room with lounge sofas and a 60-inch TV. If we can't forget about our problems in this setting, then we're worse off than I thought.

"Now I'm starting to think this was a great idea." Mike says when we, an hour later, are lying in sun-deck chairs on the beach, looking at a bunch of attractive twenty-year-olds playing beach volleyball. I have a Mojito in my right hand and Mike's enjoying some kind of umbrella drink with a lemon wedged to the glass. Mike drinks like a girl, meaning he drinks girls' drinks.

"Of course it is," I say, taking a big sip.

"You called Melody yet?" I should've known Mike isn't one to relax for five fucking minutes.

"No, I haven't. Give me a break, man. I'm trying to enjoy this."

Mike suddenly bursts out laughing, "Sleeping with your father's girlfriend, I mean that's just too much, even for you, Jack. I didn't think those things happened in real life. You should write a book or something. I got some things you can put in there too, because what's hell for us must be of entertainment value to someone."

This is why I brought Mike. Being able to see the comical side of shit that happens to you, is a first class quality in him. We toast to our misery, but as soon as I take another sip, Melody pops into my head again. I really need to call her, it's the least I can do after just bailing on her like this and I'm about to pull out my phone when a dark-haired girl, wearing mini jeans shorts on her long bronze legs, appears from out of nowhere and says in a light Spanish accent:

"Excuse me guys, but do you have a lighter?"

I'm usually a man of fast replies, especially around attractive women, but I'm so surprised by this my tongue sticks to my mouth. Mike's here though.

"Sorry, only non-smokers here," he says, not even reacting to her beauty. His relationship with Jo must have killed his penis.

"Ok, thanks anyway," she says, smiles and walks away. I give her a long look before I turn to Mike: "You saw that? She's something else." I imagine drool dripping down on my chest.

"Yes, sure. She's good looking. But please, oh please, take it easy, man. Don't start thinking about opening new doors while you're still stuck with your foot in another one. Besides, this is a typical couples resort, which means there's a 99 percent chance she has a boyfriend or husband here. So I'd strongly advise you to keep that troublemaker in your pants for once."

"But Cancun is known to be a party place, she could be here with a gang of girlfriends, possibly looking for some good times."

I say this holding my phone, the phone I was about to call Melody with, but I don't sense the irony.

"You never really stop, do you, Jack? You're here because you're running away from past mistakes! Don't tell me you're ready to dive headfirst into new ones!"

"Relax, man! I was just talking about her. Relax."

"Well, do what the fuck you want, but don't ask me to come and help you if you fuck this one up as well." Mike puts down his drink in the sand, lies back in his chair and shuts his eyes. He's tired of me and it's understandable.

I'm tired of myself too.

***

My call to Melody is short, but not very sweet. She's furious with me and has every right to be. She thinks I'm a coward and an asshole and she says she had feelings for me, but I really showed my true self now, *yada yada yada.* She tells me my poor father worries about me and she couldn't make up a believable story to save me, because she simply had no idea where I went. The good thing about this conversation is that she doesn't seem to like me anymore - instead she hates my guts.

I tell her I'll call my father right away and tell him I had to go to Cancun to help Mike battle his post-relationship depression. I know I'll need plenty of good lies to get through this one, but if there's one guy to pull that kind of thing off - it's me.

So after taking some more heat from Melody, we say goodbye and ten minutes later I call my father. I try to keep my voice calm, but I'm of course shaking with anxiety.

But my father actually sounds relieved to hear from me. I tell him I'm in Cancun and that my friend Mike has had a nervous breakdown after finding out his girlfriend cheated on him, and he needed to get away from New York, from people, from everything. I apologize and say it was really horrible of me not to text him or call him, but I was so shocked by Mike's condition I really needed to give him my full attention. It's a pretty unlikely story, but it's the best I can do and although my father doesn't sound completely convinced, he's probably still nursing his sore head and lacks the energy to question things. Instead he tells me he always wanted to go to Cancun and asks me if he should send me my bag and I reply that that would be great and give him the address of the hotel.

And that's pretty much it. He seems content with hearing I'm okay.

Afterwards, I'm so relieved I immediately call room service and order two bottles of their finest Italian wine. Is it too early to celebrate?

Time will tell.

***

We're sitting on our magnificent presidential terrace, listening to the waves of sea and drinking expensive room service wine, when Mike's phone starts vibrating and blinking like an alarm gone mad.

I instantly get a bad feeling about it and silently wish Mike not to pick it up, but of course he does and about two seconds into the conversation I know it's Joanne.

"I don't know how you could do this to me, Jo. After all I've done for you! I thought we really had something worth fighting for, but obviously you didn't." Mike drags his hand through his hair like he wants to tear it off.

"What do you mean I didn't give you enough attention? Are you fucking kidding me? I think that's all I did."

I hear the faint sound of Jo shouting on the other end.

"You know what? I only have two words for you. Fuck you. Bitch."

Mike hangs up and I'm not going to tell him that, "Fuck you, bitch," actually is three words, because I'm quite surprised and impressed by how he dealt with her.

"Congratulations, Mike! That's probably the best phone conversation I heard from you ever. Way to tell her! I'm proud of you, man." But Mike doesn't return my outstretched hand, waiting to high five. Instead he turns around and looks out across the ocean.

"I know you like to hear that, Jack. But I'm still confused. One minute I want to kill her and the next I want her back."

I don't want to start arguing with Mike now. Jo is a thing of the past and in time, he'll realize why. So I say:

"Yeah, love is hell. Now why don't you do like me and turn off your phone?" I wave my dead Blackberry at him. "Remember this is a vacation, let's treat it like one."

***

Alcohol has convinced Mike and I to head out into the Cancun nightlife. They say "what happens in Cancun, stays in Cancun," and that's the kind of carte blanche I need right now. I just wish the same goes for Coral Gables.

Cancun clubbing is quite a contrast to the yacht club party in the Gables and a strong smell of alcohol, sweat and smoke hits us as soon as we step out of the cab outside our wanted destination - the famous night club Coco Bongo. I'm known to like a party or two and I've been clubbing longer than some of the people outside the club have been alive, but for some reason the smell makes me nauseous. Mike looks only slightly more comfortable, as he usually prefers movie nights at home to these hedonistic drinking activities. He was never a party guy, and never will be. He's always overly dressed as well (today I asked him to please skip the tie), which makes him look stiff - like he wants to do taxes, not women.

"What's wrong?" he says, seeing the sick look on my face.

"I don't know, Mike, I feel like I want to throw up. Maybe the food (we had a spicy Mexican meat stew) was bad or something. Let's head inside and have a drink, maybe I'll feel better."

Coco Bongo is huge, but still packed. The crowd is mixed, but the majority of it consists of college kids going all out and all in. I feel like I'm walking around in a Girls Gone Wild video. The music is blasting so hard the floor is vibrating, as we elbow ourselves to the bar. Mike looks unimpressed.

"The music is too loud. You can't talk like this."

"It might be loud for you who haven't been out since 1999, but please stop bitching, Mike. We talk all day and now we're here to drink and enjoy ourselves. Just look for some hot girls or something while I get us some fluids."

The bar is of course filled to the rim with people trying to squeeze in and get another "complimentary" (open bar if you pay fifty dollars) drink and as in any bar on the planet the cute girls get them first. The bartenders are two sweaty Latinos who look like they might still be in high school. They're mostly occupied with having eye-to-breast contact with the half-naked college girls leaning over the bar displaying generous cleavage. It takes quite a while for one of the guys to notice me, but when his fish-eyes finally see me, the dumb look on his face tells me he won't know how to mix a decent Negroni. So I settle for a GT for me and Piña colada for Mike, plus two tequila shots to get us warmed up. Although I'm not exactly sure we need them, considering the amount of wine we've been drinking at dinner.

Seeing the milky drink in Mike's hand reminds me why I'm almost embarrassed to go out drinking with Mike - he always orders Pina Coladas or White Russians. He must have been a cow in a previous life.

We get our tequilas, pour some salt on the side of our hands, prepare the lemon, 1-2-3 and off we go. I feel a bit better after the shots and some sips of the really strong GT. I'm now confident I can make the nausea subside and drunkenness take over. I have things I need to clear on my hard drive tonight.

I also hope a few tequila shots will defrost Milky-Mike a bit, because right now he's looking like a fish out of water. I know Mike - he needs to reach a certain stage before he can enjoy a nightclub and he's not there yet.

As I down anther large sip, my mind for some reason goes to Melody. I can't help but feel sorry for her, although in a way she's as much to blame for what we did as I am. I just feel she's one of those girls who always land between a rock and a hard place, no matter how good her intentions are. I'm not too proud of being the rock, or the hard place for that matter.

We manage to drink two more tequilas each and finally Mike comes to life. His legs are trying to find the rhythm of an annoying David Guetta tune and he's failing miserably.

"Better now?" I ask him, a permanent smile now glued to his face for no reason other than being shitfaced.

"A little bit," he says with a slight drawl. "Cool place this. Some pretty hot girls too." Mike looks over to the dance floor, where there's an abundance of jumping female flesh.

"Why don't you head over there? Dance a little?" I need to stop Mike from drinking for a while now, because I'm afraid he's on the trail of over-consumption. Looking at his track record of holding strong drinks, it would result in "game over".

"What about you?" Mike slurs, and gives me a slit-eyed look.

"I'll be right here, sipping on my drink."

To my surprise, off Mike goes, milk drink in hand and a drunken groove in his step. He's feeling good now, confident for a change, which is a decent compensation for feeling shitty tomorrow.

I head to the bathroom and in the stall I stare down at my penis, silently wanting to ask it: why do you cause me so much trouble? But of course the only reply I get is a steady flow of urine. I hear the door open and some heavy footsteps behind me. I look to the left and see a beefy guy wearing a tank top, a greasy midway part and a couple of cheap-looking tattoos on his right arm. I make out an eagle in flames, some barbed wire and a few Chinese letters. The guy is a walking cliché of body ink. He's putting his left hand on the wall, like he needs it there to keep his balance. He's one of those people who desperately wants to look tough, but ends up looking silly and I bet his dick is the size of a cheese doodle. I'm squeezing out the last few drops when, from the corner of my left eye, I see the big man lose his grip on the wall, lean left, then right, and I know he's about to fall, yet I'm completely powerless. Suddenly he grabs a hold of my arm and I tumble down with him. We both hit the floor with a thud, pants half-down and his hand on my arm.

Everything seems to happen in slow motion and I guess that's how it is with all major accidents. I hear someone open the door, say "sorry!" and quickly close it (it must be quite a picture). I release myself from the drunken muscle man and pull up my pants. I stand up slowly, but the guy's not moving. I don't know if the fall knocked him out, because his eyes are closed. For a second I pray I don't have to give him the mouth to mouth, as it would make the experience even creepier.

"Hey!" I shout twice and after the second time his eyes open. I reach out my hand to him and using all my strength, I manage to get him up to a standing position. His pants are still down (it was more of a jumbo shrimp than a cheese doodle by the way), but he comes alive enough to pull them up.

"I think you better head home, buddy," I say, quite calm despite what just happened.

"Mmmhmmhgggghhhhffff," he says as I help him out of the bathroom. When we come out we have a small crowd looking at us. We might now be known as the weirdest gay couple in Cancun, which means I really have to take comfort in the "what stays here" bit.

I hear someone saying, "John," in a worried voice, and a woman with stripy blonde hair and an 80s tanning bed tan comes up to us. She wears too much make-up, especially around her eyes. I think she's in her upper forties, which means she could be either his mother or his girlfriend.

"John," she says again. I hand this John over to her and she helps him outside and out of my sight.

I head out to the dance floor in hope that the people involved, myself included, will quickly forget about the bathroom incident. I spot Mike talking and trying to dance with a freckled strawberry blonde. It almost looks like he's using her small frame as a crutch to avoid falling over. He's too drunk now for any kind of romantic action, but hopefully he's having a good time at least.

I decide to leave Mike alone for now and head back to the bar again. I'm just about ready to order my drink when I see her, my Latina dream. She's standing over at the other end of the bar, talking to some ugly-looking guy with shiny and spiky hair. Who can it be? Her boyfriend? That would be one unevenly balanced couple, I think to myself.

Well, there's only one way to find out...

"Got light?" I shout to her, probably sounding drunker than I am.

"Sorry?" she shouts back, although I'm not sure she recognizes me, which is a bad sign.

"Got a lighter?" I try again and I'm now getting closer to her with a stupid smile on my face. This of course also nets the attention of her boyfriend/brother/friend who's giving me an annoyed stare.

"Sure," she says and starts looking around in her purse. No recollection though - is my face not pretty enough to remember?

"I don't really need one," I say as she hands me her pink lighter and now I really sound like an idiot. "I mean, aren't you the girl who asked me and my friend for a lighter at the beach earlier?"

Her eyes light up. And there it is, the smile that makes angels sing. "I just thought you were some guy looking for a lighter," she says innocently, while I think: No, I am just some guy looking to get laid. But what I say is:

"I was just trying to be funny! What a nice coincidence to meet again, like there's only one nightclub in Cancun." I'm trying to make it sound like I'm not hitting on her, but I guess it's obvious, as I can't think of one man in his right mind who wouldn't.

"But this is the best one! I love this place. My brother and I have gone here three nights in a row!" Good news! *Brodder*, her accent a lovely Spanglish, almost as juicy as her lips.

She puts her arm around the guy behind her. He looks un-amused by being introduced to guy-hitting-on-his-sister number 1043.

"Jack," I say as friendly as possible, "nice to meet you."

"Rico," he replies, hardly even looking at me. Rico is skinny and lethargic, but I should probably not read his facial expression to mean he doesn't care whether someone tries to score with his sister or not, because that's not what they say about Latino men. I need to play my cards well here.

"So you're here on a family vacation or? Where are you guys from?" This comes out a bit more slurry than I intended. I'm not in hundred percent control of my voice, but I hope she doesn't notice.

"We're from Mexico City actually and I guess you could say it's kind of a family vacation. We decided to take our parents to Cancun on their 30th anniversary. They actually got married here 30 years ago! I'm Cristina by the way." She stretches out a small, delicate hand. Normally I would be cheeky enough to kiss it, but not with her brother in the sidelines.

"Nice to meet you, Cristina. I'm Jack, as I just said, and I'm on vacation with my friend Mike, who's somewhere around here." I point towards the dance floor. Hopefully Mike is still standing on it.

I tell Cristina I'm from New York and I work with advertising in an agency I co-founded. I learn that she studied in California for a year (which is why her English is so good) but she's never been to New York, which I obviously follow up with "you have to go!" meaning: come with me! We small talk, half-shouting over the music while her brother mostly stands there with a bored look on his face, sipping on a Sol beer. He's stuck to his sister like a leech, which makes it difficult for me to talk and flirt freely.

I feel someone touch my shoulder and turn around to find Mike, semi-conscious. "I...I...think I need to go," he says and you could tell he's fighting back vomit.

With a glued-on brother and a sideways Mike on my hands, I can't win any lady battles tonight, so I wave the white flag and just hope I get another chance to win this beautiful woman's heart.

"I think we have to leave," I say, nodding towards Mike, "but it was very nice talking you. Is there any way I can see you again?" This is a shot in the dark, of course, but it's strange how often it works like a charm.

"Sure," she says and takes out a white Samsung mobile from her teal-colored purse. "You can give me your number and I'll text you when I'm out next time or if we get a coffee or something."

My heart makes a little jump as I carefully give her my number and make sure she puts it in correctly, despite Mike breathing toxins in my ear. I smile and repeat how I would love to see her again and then I wave goodbye. Mike and I head out onto the pavement where he throws up against the wall. It's mostly a liquid vomit, but enough to make people walking by turn their faces in disgust.

"Attaboy," I say. "Hard drive cleared."

Then I hail a cab.

***

The next day doesn't start until lunchtime and it starts badly. I'm woken up by a tiny drummer playing a solo in the back of my head. Hearing Mike throw up in the toilet, flushing, then throwing up again, doesn't exactly help - feeling better than him is slim comfort in Hangovertown.

"What's up, Mikey?" I shout from the living room of our presidential suite.

"Everything," he says, weakly.

"I'm going to order some aspirin - you'll feel better in no-time." I shout back to him and then I call room service, place the order and go to our mini-bar and pick up two small bottles of sparkling water, a coke and an outrageously expensive miniature can of Macadamia nuts, sit down on the sofa and turn on the TV. This is going to be a long and slow day.

After a while Mike comes out from the bathroom, looking like he was just raped by a werewolf. His hair is on end, his eyes are red and his face is pink-ish. He burps and scratches his ass. He's a sight for sore eyes and the sorer they'll be when they see him.

"Rough night, huh?" I say and smile at him.

"Uggghhhhuh," Mike sounds like a distant relative of Chewbacca.

"Don't worry about it, your buddy Jack here has ordered some medicine to lift that mean concrete helmet of yours." I've noticed it's far easier to sound upbeat when someone is feeling worse than you.

"Great," he says and dives onto the sofa, mumbling something about wanting to die.

A night like the one before usually leaves a Swiss cheese full of memory holes, but not this time. Cristina's hauntingly beautiful eyes and killer legs stand out like someone carved them into my retina. I have to see this girl again, I really have to, but of course the ball is in her hands now. Will she call? I have a feeling she will, but then again I'm not used to getting turned down and there's a first time for everything.

Three gentle knocks on the door means room service. The room service guy is in his early twenties and looks intimidated when I open the door, but I probably provide a nasty appearance today, not having slept well. He hands me a package of aspirin on a silver tray, which is a nice but exaggerated presentation for standard pharmaceuticals. I take the package, give him a ten-dollar bill and say "gracias". It might not be a lot of tips for someone living in this kind of suite, but I don't care. I hate tips - I never get any myself.

After a few minutes in silence, sipping coke and downing aspirins, Mike wakes up.

"What happened with that girl you were hitting on?" he says, taking me by surprise. I didn't think he would remember much of the evening.

"Nothing really, we just talked. Her brother was standing next to her so I took it easy. She got my number though, so we'll see if she calls or not." I try to say this as casually as possible, because I know Mike's unimpressed by my unwillingness to surrender the chase of the opposite sex, no matter what trouble it brings me.

"So you're really ready to meet more women?" Mike has a mix of disbelief and disgust in his voice.

"Melody was a mistake, I admit that. I don't know what I was thinking. This girl, she's something else, she's special."

"You also said that Melody was special," Mike replies instantly. Isn't he hung-over? Where does he get the energy to interrogate me like this?

"Well, Melody is a very nice girl, but she's also my father's girlfriend."

"Yeah, I know, what I don't understand is how you couldn't see that before you decided to sleep with her?" Mike has an obvious distaste for the cheating kind and we can all understand why.

"Okay, I sometimes think with my genitalia - get over it. I can't turn back time so I might as well move on with my life."

"It might seem that easy to you, Jack, but you hurt people, you play with them. You have probably hurt many women in your life and you just don't seem to give a shit."

"That's bullshit, Mike, of course I care. I don't like to be an asshole, but I can't stay with someone I don't love either. That would be unfair to both of us."

I'm starting to get seriously pissed with Mike's attitude towards me. It's old and I'm tired.

"I don't know who the right girl is for you, there seems to be something wrong with every girl you meet. It's either their personalities, something in their looks, something about their friends, about their relatives, whatever. You're just afraid to commit."

My blood is now officially at a boil. "What the fuck is this, Mike? We're in Cancun, we're on holiday, we're tired as fuck and you give me all this shit! I mean, give me a fucking break!"

Mike and I, we're like an old married couple, we have arguments, we shout at each other. He's often right, but I also want to think I give him direction sometimes. This is friendship. So he shouldn't be too surprised I'm now angry enough to take the remote control and throw it at the flat screen TV in the room and smash it.

Then I take a cold shower.

***

It takes a while before we speak again. Mike is clearly disturbed by my breaking of the presidential TV and I'm just frustrated with his image of me. Is this what people think? That I'm a cold, heart-breaking bastard, incapable of love? If my best friend believes that, what do other people think? I wasn't ready for Mike's attack and although there might be some truth to what he's saying (he knows me best after all), he didn't have to provoke me. He should know my temper by now.

After the long shower I go to my bedroom and just lay there, look up at the ceiling and let myself soak in a dangerous mix of self-pity and loathing. Not even my best friend wants to hang out with me – I don't think I've ever felt this lonely before. I spend half an hour of restless thinking about my past, about the few "serious" relationships I've had, Jenny, Krista, Heather, all ended by me by fading out over a few weeks and then just breaking them off. I see the same pattern in all of them now. I like the wooing part and the passion of the unknown love, so I shower my victims with affection, cook my own candlelight dinners, buy gifts and flowers, I do everything romantic except for writing my own poems. Then, when they have fallen badly for me, I get bored or maybe scared and somehow manage to detach myself emotionally and break their hearts. That's what I seem to do, time and time again.

I try to think back on all my one-nighters, two-nighters, and weeks of bliss with girls I've had, but it's all a blur. The blend of alcohol and stress has apparently been a powerful eraser of memories.

Or were the moments not powerful enough to even become memories?

Maybe I really am afraid of relinquishing the freedom of single life? Is this what Mike means? I guess I could ask him, because he stands by my door now, looking fresher and ready to be human again.

"I'm sorry," he says, "I was tired and had a headache, I know I went too far."

"I thought you were maybe stepping on the gas a little hard. But that's okay, I understand you, I have a knack of annoying people. Besides, I've been thinking a bit. Maybe you're right - maybe I'm afraid of committing to a relationship. I seem to make the same mistake over and over again, that's for sure."

"Well, you're not alone in finding relationships difficult, Jack. I just think you need to give them a chance and not give up so soon. But who am I to criticize you? I'm single myself after three years with a woman I thought really loved me as much as I did her. So I can't really offer expert advice." Mike shrugs and then continues:

"How long have we known each other now? 12 years? The good old university days. I remember how impressed I was with your confidence - with women, in school. You thought you were the king of the world or that it just was a question of time until you became and I really liked that, I wanted that. I almost thought that by hanging out with you the confidence would rub off on me. Maybe it did a little, maybe it didn't. Probably we're just too different."

"We're not in college anymore - in fact 40 isn't far away and sometimes it scares the shit out of me. I know I don't want to grow old alone and I don't think you want to do that either. I'm starting to realize my relationship with Joanne wasn't perfect by any stretch of the imagination, but I still miss being in a relationship. I feel completely confused as a single man and I'm afraid I'll never find the right woman for me. It's terrifying - more terrifying than losing Joanne."

"For you, Jack, it's different. You know how to meet women - you could probably find one for every day of the week. But this is the first time I've seen you like this - doubting yourself and your actions and at first I was like Holy shit! What's wrong with him? But now

I'm thinking, maybe it's not such a bad thing? Maybe it's just growing up?"

Mike's monologue has ended and although interesting, he's in a far too philosophical mode for me. So I say:

"Can we finish this talk while eating? I'm dying for a burger."

***

After a grease-filled dinner and two giant cokes, followed by double espressos, we take a walk on the beach. Two guys living in a suite together, eating in the hotel restaurant together, walking the beach together, yeah it might be a bit strange, but it's the kind of friendship we both need right now, someone to look after you in the crisis you're going through.

It's windy today and the windsurfers are still out, trying to catch the last big waves of the day, creating a serene image. We sit down in the cool sand and watch the orange sun being slowly dipped into the sea. We're both too tired to talk. The only thing right now that can keep me in a hopeful mood is Cristina, and that's why my head is going back and forth trying to spot her, although I understand the odds are not exactly on my side.

"You're looking for her, right?" Mike reads my mind.

"Yes, I know it seems desperate, but I would really like to see her again. She would take my mind of...of...things."

"If she wants to see you again she'll call. Relax and enjoy the sunset."

"But what if she lost my number?"

Mike seems amused by my insecurity, "Maybe you really like this girl, because you sound like one yourself. If it's meant to happen, it happens. You know what you should do instead of worrying like this? Go and get us a new TV."

***

The hotel is not happy with me breaking a 2000-dollar TV. I tell them they can deduct it from my card and for a second I almost feel like a rock star, but that's just for a second because then I feel like a psycho again. When I tell the hotel manager it was an accident he just lifts his left eyebrow slightly, mutters something in Spanish and looks deeply unconvinced. I have no excuse, neither real nor invented, so I let my credit card do the talking instead.

While I'm waiting for my card to be swiped, the text from Cristina arrives. She wonders if I want to meet up for lunch somewhere tomorrow and as I'm reading the message, I feel giddy like a little girl. I reply that it sounds great, although just after I click the send-button I realize I'd already agreed with Mike to go sightseeing to Chichen Itzá, the famous archeological site which rates as one of the seven wonders of the world. I agreed to tag along when I had nothing better to do and now I have. I hate blowing him off, especially now when we're getting closer, but he knows my priorities. A beautiful woman is more of a wonder for me than any house or landmark will ever be.

***

As I'm combing my black hair backwards, I realize I'm actually a bit nervous about this lunch and that's rare. Maybe it's because I've decided it will be the launch of the new, more responsible me, and I'll do my absolute best to get this one right. I take a break from my grooming and gulp down some whisky. I need to still my nerves, but not too much.

I dress in a black linen shirt and beige linen trousers, thinking that linen speaks relaxed and casual, yet elegant (okay, I didn't have an abundance of choice), and I want Cristina to feel trust, to see the reliable and nice Jack, not the one who drinks too much, sleeps around, puts work before anything and has a broken moral compass.

That's the person I want to kill on this trip - long live, the new and improved Jack!

I'm supposed to meet her downtown in some local Mexican restaurant, which she said was very good, and I'm going to get there early, which is another new feature in Jack 2.0.

I'm in fact so early I end up sitting alone on the back terrace, slowly sipping on a Mojito that's way too sweet for my taste. The restaurant is indeed typically Mexican, bathing in pastel colors and dark wood and it does look a bit dirty. It's not a place I would have chosen myself, but I will trust Cristina's judgment and stay positive. The terrace is in a great location though and if I raise my head a bit I can see the beach and the sea, so that's mostly what I'm doing until Cristina appears, looking absolutely amazing in hot-pants-sized jeans shorts and a black top. She has let her long, thick and wavy hair hang out, which is even more attractive than the ponytail. My heartbeat accelerates.

"Hi Jack," Cristina looks down on her small gold watch, "sorry, have you been waiting?"

All my life, I think, and scold myself for being cheesy, but all I say is "no, not at all."

***

The food in the restaurant is nothing special (or maybe I ordered the wrong dish), but the company is. Cristina's dark-brown eyes are sparkling and she speaks with intelligence and confidence, and I don't get the feeling for one minute that she understands how beautiful she is, something which makes me even more attracted to her. We're sharing a second bottle of white Chardonnay and the ice has since long been broken. We're actually already talking like old friends, sharing stories, laughter, and I'm so relaxed with her, I've forgotten all about being my new self and not talking too much. Instead words are pouring from my mouth along with compliments and attempts to get lingering eye contact, and I'm at least aware of myself enough to know that I'm falling head over heels for her.

There's something about how she speaks, the way she seems to end every sentence with a smile, that's totally spellbinding. Her voice is very soft and womanly, but it's not unsteady or unsure, and her attitude to life is so matter-of-fact, positive, and honest, I'm convinced she's the love of my life. Deep down I know it's too soon to tell, but I already feel that if there's a time where I need to give my everything to someone, then it's now. And it's the thought of starting with no secrets which makes me tell her everything, why I lost my appetite for my job, how I hit a wall, why I came here, pretty much all of it, except for my affair with Melody of course.

Although I'm engrossed in my own story (yes, I'm quite the narcissist), I'm watching Cristina closely, studying her reactions. Women rarely like to see weakness in men and I'm afraid talking about my breakdown will put her off. But Cristina just looks at me and says:

"Isn't life great though? The way there's always a chance to start over, to see things differently, to look back and learn?"

I want to kiss her right there and then, but I know it's too soon, too risky.

"I thought you'd think I was crazy or something, but I didn't want to hide anything either. I try to be an honest person."

"You've just opened your heart and soul to me, Jack. It's not crazy, it's quite wonderful."

I've opened my heart to Cristina and I'm dying for her to open hers. The only thing I know about her is that she's doing accounting for the family company, which is selling handmade Mexican pine furniture. Not exactly the kind of things I'm most interested in.

She also tells me we must come from very different family backgrounds, because she's very close to her family and especially her father, Salvador. She says she really believes in the strength of the family and it's sad I don't have the same connection to my family members, that she has to hers. "Maybe family is not as important in America?" she asks.

"I don't know. From my own experience I would say no, but family values are quite strong in general, I think. At least in theory."

"In Mexico (Mehico – again loving the accent), you rarely hear about a family like yours. Family is the most important thing you have, it's what you depend on, it's your source of strength and inspiration. I don't understand this American thing of always putting work first. Your parents are what gave you life, who raised you, how can you not be close to them?"

Cristina fiddles with a lock of hair and she's slightly excited about the discussion.

"I was doing fine in America, the country has many benefits of course, and my studies were going well. I think I had a bright future there, but when my family asked me to move back - when they needed my help - I just had to go. My family is everything to me."

"But if you were doing well over there, isn't it a bit selfish of your family to ask you to move back? I mean, isn't your family also supposed to support you in building your life, in fulfilling your dreams?"

"I think careers are incredibly selfish. It's all about self-fulfillment, ego boosting, it's all about you, you, you. I think you cannot value life only in success. I actually never regret moving back - I'm happy in Mexico City, living with my family, helping them with the business. I feel like I'm apart of something bigger, it's the natural place for me to be."

"But you wouldn't consider living in the States again? If an opportunity arose?" This is of course an important question if what I think could be a relationship is ever going to work, so I might as well get it out of the way.

Cristina seems to study her delicate hands.

"I don't know. I don't think so, but I guess it depends on the situation." She sends me a shy smile.

Cristina has this strong force inside of her - a fiery passion for life - which rubs off on you. I've never ever seen anything like it and after three hours of deep and honest conversation, something's blasting inside of me that she is the one to turn my own downward spiral around, and I can't see our meeting as a coincidence. She's here to save me. The question is what I can do for her.

Suddenly she stops midway through a sentence, "Oh, I'm already late. I promised my father I would be home at four. I'm very sorry, this has been so nice."

My heart sinks, but when she reaches out and grabs my hand, it floats up again.

"Do you mind if I walk with you to your hotel?" I ask.

"Of course not, I would very much like you to."

When we're outside her hotel and about to say goodbye, it's one of those awkward moments where you don't know if you should kiss, hug, shake hands or just say goodbye.

"I had a really good time, Jack."

"Me too. When can I see you again?" This sounds a bit forced, but I need to know when. I'm not letting this woman go.

"I don't know, maybe tonight? We could go out for dinner if you like?" My heart leaps and spins and my face breaks out into a grin.

"Sounds great. Should I pick you up at your hotel?"

"Yeah, why don't you come here at eight? I have to go now." Then she leans up and kisses me on the cheek. It's a sweet and loving gesture and so fitting for the moment, for the whole afternoon.

Cristina waves at me as she's walking towards the doors of the hotel lobby. I wave back at her and feel like 15 years old again. Although I can't remember ever feeling like this when I was 15 - my whole body buzzing with excitement. So I start walking back to my hotel, very excited to tell Mike about what a fantastic day I've had.

But when I get back to the hotel I learn that the day might not be so fantastic after all. Standing by the reception desk is...drumroll...(how much did I drink at lunch?) my father and Melody.

"Dad? What are you doing here? What's going on?" I sound terrified, because I am. My father turns around with a big smile on his face, walks up to me, gives me a hug and the mandatory three stinging slaps on the back.

"Surprise!" He chuckles loudly. "Are you shocked? I didn't mean to scare you, son. When I was looking at different shipping options, Melody came up with the idea of delivering your luggage personally and at the same time combining it with a nice vacation." My father grabs Melody's ass and kisses her on the cheek, "That's my girl," he says. Then he looks at me, and smiles and points to my suitcase, which is standing there on the floor, mocking me.

Melody comes up to me and puts her arms around my neck. She's wearing a short yellow dress and her breasts are about to jump out of it as she presses them against me hard.

"Nice to see you again, Jack," she says, while I'm too shocked to say anything. My wheels are coming off. Here I was just about to tell Mike about my newfound love and now I need to tell him we have trouble on our hands.

I don't know what devious plan Melody has come up with to suggest a trip to see me, but I'm starting to realize I'm far from out of the woods yet.

I manage to squeeze out some words.

"This is really a great surprise and it's very nice to see you guys. I'm going to head up to my room now, but I guess I'll see you a bit later then?" I try to sound normal.

"We're just going to drop our bags and freshen up, and then we can head over to your room. Which number are you in?"

"One of the presidential suites. The left wing."

"That's my boy," my father says and laughs.

There went the vacation and my peace of mind in one go.

Mike is lying in the sofa, watching "our" new TV, when I enter the suite.

"So how was your day?" he says, not even looking at me. He's likely in a sulk for me not tagging along to see old historical things.

"It was fantastic, I mean really fantastic. What a woman! I was on a pink cloud. At least until I met my father and Melody in the lobby."

"What?" Mike's not sulking anymore.

"Seems like they thought it a good idea to deliver my luggage in person, with a surprise fucking visit."

"They're here now? In this hotel?"

"Yes, and what's extra great about it is that the whole thing is her idea, can you believe it? There's something very strange about this, Mike, something very unsettling. Why would she do this after what went on between us? Last time we talked she told me she hated me."

"I have no idea, except it does sound like trouble."

"I need a drink," I say and head over to the mini-bar.

"Make me one too." Mike calls from the sofa.

As I gulp down the tumbler of whisky, I can't help but feel that the consequences of my actions are about to catch up with me and I can't do a damn thing about it.

***

My father is standing on our terrace, admiring the view. He's so tan he's Lobster man - a warning symbol in nature.

Melody is also here of course, looking out on the sea, saying very little.

"I should have booked us a room like this, or what do you think, Mel?" he says, stuffing his hands in his chinos and walking around the room.

I'm just watching this from the sofa, slightly shell-shocked, while sipping my third large tumbler of whisky. My mouth has mostly been shooting out empty phrases, because I need to leave my head out of this.

"How is the nightlife here? I mean, what happens in Cancun stays in Cancun, right?" My father winks. He is, like always, in good spirits.

"I sure hope it does," Mike says and gives me a look.

"You guys want to join me and Mel for dinner later? We're just going to take a walk and maybe have drink and then we can meet up. What do you say, maybe around eight?" My father says in the voice of someone who's used to getting what he wants.

My brain is processing the information like a drunken boxer would a recently received blow, and before I manage to reply Mike says "sure," not yet knowing about my dinner plans with Cristina.

I'm too distraught to say anything and when my father and Melody finally leave our room, Mike turns to me and says: "So, that didn't go that badly, at least he doesn't know."

"It went to hell, Mike. I have a dinner booked with Cristina tonight and I really must see her again. This double booking is the worst possible turn of events - I can't cancel on Cristina and how can I cancel on my father? How would I explain something like that? I don't see what lie could help me here."

"Well, can't you see Cristina tomorrow instead? Tell her other plans got in the way? That you got sick or something?"

"I can't do that. What if she sees me out? I don't want to blow it with this woman, Mike, nobody has ever made me feel this good before. I really have to see her tonight."

Mike frowns, "You certainly know how to make life difficult for yourself."

In the end Mike convinces me to call Cristina and explain the situation. I have to postpone our dinner date - it's the only reasonable thing to do.

"Hi Cristina, it's Jack. How are you?" My voice is shaking.

"Hi Jack! I'm good thanks, sitting on the terrace, talking to my father and sipping on a glass of wine."

"Sounds great. About the dinner, you won't believe this, but my father just surprised me by coming here and now he wants to go out to eat tonight. Do you think we can postpone until tomorrow? He really wants to see me and I don't want to disappoint him after he went through all the trouble to come here. Maybe we can meet for drinks later?"

Cristina thinks for what feels like a long time.

"Yes, of course no problem, but I was actually talking to my parents just now and they would really like to meet you. Wouldn't it be nice if we all have dinner together? Now that we're all here."

Cristina sounds super excited about this, while I consider jumping from the terrace right this minute. Meeting the parents on the second date - that's what I would usually label as a major disaster for any relationship. Parents meeting parents? Even crazier! Object of affection meeting previous lay on second date? Too ridiculous to comment on! Still I find no other option than to say yes, because some mentally damaged part of me thinks I need to show an interest in family to really win Cristina over, even if it means saying yes to the dinner date from hell.

"How did it go?" Mike is eager to know as soon as I head back inside the suite again.

"It went fan-fucking-tastic! Now we're all going to dinner together, Cristina's family, my father, Melody and you. I guess I could just go and shoot myself right away. It's faster, less torture."

Mike breaks out laughing and bends over the sofa, his face all red.

"What's so fucking funny? I'm dying here and you're laughing at me?"

"Sorry, sorry," Mike tries to get his act together, "but you must be a real masochist my friend, because every time you have the chance to get out of trouble, you make it ten times worse! Why didn't you just say no or invent some lie? You work in advertising - you lie and create stories for a living!" He laughs some more and then continues:

"I just think it will be really interesting to see how Melody reacts when she finds out it only took you a couple of days to forget about her and hook up with a new girl. Cheers to that."

And in reply I raise my glass and mock-toast to my own misery.

***

There's a wide variety of facial expressions in the lobby of the Fiesta Americana Coral Beach. Cristina seems very happy to have Lobster man and Barbie girl present for our dinner and by the way looks astonishing in her red skin-tight dress with a slit that makes her legs reach up into infinity. Her parents, Carmen and Salvador, are both impeccably dressed and reek of power and riches. They look suspiciously at me as I stretch out my hand and introduce myself. I understand them though. To them I'm just an older gringo taking an unwanted interest in their daughter. There's a chance I smell of alcohol too, although I'm still too awkward and nervous to get drunk. But that's probably a good thing if I want to make any kind of positive impression on them.

My father is of course positive to the larger crowd in his "the more the merrier"-kind of way, but what Melody thinks of all this I can just guess, although I don't think she's very merry.

I really have my work cut out for me tonight, ignoring Melody's likely boiling anger while focusing on Cristina and making her parents feel comfortable around me.

Cristina's father Salvador will definitely be hard to impress. His eyes are like burning pieces of coal and his eyebrows are thick and black with some white strands in them - signs of gentle aging. He's a big, broad-shouldered and confident man with a loud, dominating voice.

His wife Carmen is basically a 20-year-older version of Cristina. She's elegant in a tasteful black cocktail dress and wears a lot - but not too much - make-up. She's almost regal in her ways.

The only piece in the Gonzalez family puzzle I cannot squeeze in, is Rico. He's more of a guy you find on the street, selling bags of cocaine, hanging out in shady neighborhoods and inspecting rims on lowered-down cars with his tattooed buddies. He seems completely uninterested in the normal proceedings of life and his apathy scares me. He gives me the dead fish handshake and then throws a half-interested look at Melody's bouncy cleavage. It's the only real sign of life in him so far.

Understandably, we're all a bit confused and nervous about this family blind date, everyone except for Cristina and my father, who both are remarkably relaxed and positive. It's something in their nature, I guess. Mike mostly seems amused - this is a show for him now, a show he's able to watch from the best possible seat.

My plan for getting through this testing evening is giving almost all my attention to Cristina and not to throw as much as a glance over towards Melody. I don't know what her intentions were for coming here, but she couldn't have expected this and now I'm afraid she might do something we'll all regret, like making a scene and/or tell my father about our brief encounter. I need to have a one-on-one with her before this evening's over, but not here, not now.

My head is racing as the group splits into two stretch-limos. The Gonzalez apparently travel only in style. In the car Cristina informs me we're going to a place called La Habichuela, a famous Cancun restaurant and that I have to try their specialty, which somehow involves a coconut. I smile at her when she says this, doing my best to mask my bubbling uneasiness.

The drinks couldn't arrive fast enough. We're sitting at two pushed-together round tables in the back garden of the cozy restaurant and the mood is awkward. The only people talking are my father and Salvador. I don't know what they're talking about, but they seem to be getting along pretty well. My father gets along with everyone though.

Mike has tried to start a conversation with Melody, maybe to divert her attention, but possibly also because she seems to be the first woman in a while he finds attractive. Melody's mood is icy, but he keeps trying and I know I owe him for it. Weird brother Rico is tapping on his cell phone and the only person he's said a word to so far is his mother.

"It's really nice this place," I say and look lovingly at Cristina.

"Yes, the food is fantastic. Remember now to order the Cocochuela, it's what they're famous for." Although I'm not exactly hungry and not much into either seafood or coconuts, I tell her I will.

Finally the drinks arrive, in the form of a few cocktails and a couple of bottles of wine. I could drink them all and still be walking on nails.

My father surprises me by telling a story I haven't heard before, a story about how he went to Mexico City with a few friends many years ago (during his freewheeling single days) and got completely lost trying to find a hotel. After walking around until his feet bled, he ended up in a poor area where they had this huge street party with live music and where no one spoke English. He ended up befriending one of the families at the party and spent the night on their broken and dog-bitten old couch after drinking too much tequila. He says he had one of the best nights of his life there and I believe him.

The story and the way my father tells it actually makes the whole table (including Rico) laugh, and I silently thank the lord for my father's professional ice-breaking skills. Selling real-estate has made him into a conversational master.

The mood improves along with the alcohol intake and I think even Cristina starts to get a bit tipsy, because her hand is touching my left thigh. This is great of course but what's even better is that Mike's finally starting to get through to Melody. He can be a funny guy when in the mood and I'm really happy he's on his best behavior tonight.

We're finishing a really sweet ice cream dessert when my father suddenly rises from the table and lifts his glass. He mock-coughs a bit to make sure he has everyone's attention. His eyes are a bit unsteady from all the wine he's been drinking, but he seems keen on getting something off of his chest.

"I want to say a few things. Firstly, I want to congratulate you, Salvador, Carmen, Rico and Cristina, on an excellent choice of restaurant, because the food is truly amazing." He pauses. "Then I want to say something about marriage and relationships, because it's surely a great triumph for love that Salvador and Carmen are celebrating their 30th anniversary here in Cancun! Cheers to them!" He raises his glass towards Cristina's parents and we all stand up and raise ours in a toast.

"Staying on the subject of love, I have a small announcement to make." My father makes a pause, gathering steam for the finish. "Although we haven't been together long, I figured, actually we both figured, that life is short and when something feels as good as this does, you're a fool not to celebrate it. And that's why my beautiful girlfriend Melody," now he points the glass towards Melody, who looks at him with a slightly tired smile, "and I are getting married. The wedding will take place in Coral Gables in six weeks and you're all very welcome if you can make it. So I hope you can join me in a toast to that!"

Whoa! My 60-year-old father is getting married to this 29-year-old ex-stripper who has already cheated on him (not that he knows of course). When and how did this happen and why does he have to announce it like this, without talking to me first?

We all stand up and toast to their happiness and I look over at Melody, but her eyes are everywhere except at me. I really need to talk to her to figure out what the hell is going on here. I'm suddenly angry with her for cheating on my father (even though it was with me!) and then wanting to marry him. And why doesn't she look happy about it? I mean, you better think twice before agreeing to marry a man double your age, right? Is she after the money? Well, with my father's health he'll outlive all the cockroaches of the world - so no luck there!

I'm so lost in thought I hardly notice Salvador standing behind me. He wants to have a word he says. Surprised, I nod and we both walk silently out of the garden while the others are talking about my father's wedding plans. When we're out in front of the restaurant I get an image into my head of Salvador taking out a gun and shooting me in the street. But when he digs his hand into his jacket pocket he doesn't bring out a gun, but instead a thin gold box containing a couple of thick and expensive-looking cigars. The way he opens the box, picks up the cigar, smells it and cuts with his pocket knife, which appears, as it seems, from nowhere, tells me he has performed these motions many times. It's all seamless and elegant and I notice that for a big man, Salvador has quite delicate hands, not something I expected considering he spent most of his life in the furniture business.

"These are from the Dominican Republic and in my opinion the best cigars in the world." This is as much as he's said to me throughout the whole dinner, but he's been busy with my dad of course. He hands me the cigar and brings out a matching gold lighter and lights it up for me. I don't feel much like smoking, but saying no could end with sudden death. That's how it feels at least.

The first puff is so strong I'm almost about to cough, but I manage to fight it off, as I don't want to look unmanly in front of Salvador.

"You know, Jack, I'm not a stupid man." Salvador's accent is very heavy so I have to listen really carefully. "I know you like Cristina and from what I hear she likes you too. I don't want anyone to take my little girl away from me, but in the end she's her own woman, always has been, and she decides. That's life, no? So I just want you to know that you seem like a good man to me and your father does too and if you and Cristina want to be together, I will treat you as family." Salvador gives me a crooked smile, he knows he made a movie-like speech and he enjoyed it, but he's not quite finished, "But I also have to say that if you hurt my baby girl I will treat you as the enemy, and it's no fun being an enemy of a Gonzalez."

I don't know what I expected him to say, but I didn't expect him to threaten me. I react the only way I could and tell him I will never hurt Cristina. Although how could I know, since I have a decent track record of hurting women in the past.

I had hoped our talk would be over, but it's not.

"Where do you see yourself, Jack? You're from New York, right?"

"Where I see myself? I don't really understand the question."

"If you and Cristina are going to be together, I would like you to live in Mexico City. As you know Cristina works in the family business and I cannot afford to lose her. Not only for the business of course, what I'm saying is I can't live hundreds of miles away from her. So if you're serious about things and want to live a life in Mexico, I can set you up with a job, no problem. I have plenty of contacts."

"That's a very kind offer, Salvador." But it's not really kind, it's disturbing. Does a relationship with Cristina automatically equal a move to Mexico City?

"I'm glad you understand. We haven't talked a lot, Jack, but my feeling about you is good. I take many decisions in my life on gut feeling and it's usually right. I hope I'm right about you too."

Then without further ado he throws his cigar on the ground, stomps on it casually, puts his big hand on my shoulder and says:

"Let's go in and have a brandy."

When we return to the table the mood is cheerful, which is the opposite of what I'm feeling. My talk with Salvador has made my heart sink down to my shoes. Cristina looks very happy when I sit down next to her, but I'm not really there anymore, I'm lost in thought, speeding away on my own emotional roller coaster ride. Suddenly I'm overcome with guilt and sadness, all the anxiety from recent weeks resurfacing at once.

Cristina leans over, "You're so quiet, is something wrong? Was it something my father said?"

"Nah, I'm just a bit tired. Your father's nice, he just said he likes me. If I get an espresso, I'll be alright." I force a smile.

"Okay, let's order some coffees then. And I knew he'd like you, but let me tell you, it's not that easy to get his approval."

"Good, that's great to hear." I say from a mental distance.

Then Cristina takes my hand, squeezes it and I feel a little better. Where we go from here is anybody's guess.

***

When we take the taxis back to the hotel everybody, except for myself, is pretty hammered - even Melody seems strangely upbeat. Before we split up into different cars, Cristina kisses me on the mouth. It's the first actual kiss and it's great, but I'm not as excited by it as I should be, because my head is still elsewhere.

The Gonzalez are all going to their hotel and we're going to ours. I would normally try to find a way for Cristina and I to spend the night together, but despite how weird it might sound to you (because it does to me), sex isn't on my mind right now.

Melody seems completely uninterested in Cristina and I, instead she's occupied with Mike, who seems to have thrown all caution to the wind and is pretty much hitting on her. My father doesn't notice, because he seems to be fighting an urge to either throw up some Mexican food or fall asleep. I'm starting to wonder what was really in those drinks we had.

From the depths of my father's drunken abyss he speaks, "What nice people!" Burp, "and what a girl you have there in Cristina. Don't let a girl like that go. Ever." My father's breath could kill any fly in the vicinity.

"Yeah," I say, trying to sound as nonchalant as possible, since I'm not really in the mood of talking to drunken people, even if it's my father. Also, Melody has finally let go of Mike's attention and is now staring at me with contempt in her eyes. Dad doesn't notice any of this though - he just rambles on.

"But if you want her, you must show it, you must be ready to sacrifice that comfortable bachelor lifestyle of yours. Life is about finding real love and if you find it you have to follow it, no matter if it takes you to the end of the world." Dad kisses Melody on the cheek and then burps again, giving the limo a malicious smell.

Sacrifice? What's he talking about? Moving to Mexico? I have to assume Salvador has already sold him on the idea. I can't believe two 60-year-olds are making the decision of where I should live my life. Moving to another country is a big thing, a huge thing, and you don't make decisions like that after only a few days together.

Or do you? I'm confused.

We reach our hotel. Melody helps my father out of the car and when she does I'm again reminded of their ridiculous age difference. My father really looks old as he uses Melody's small frame to get out of the taxi, his drunken red face doesn't make this any less noticeable of course. He staggers over to me and hugs me, basically resting his large body against mine and whispers he's so happy I finally found someone and what a great "gal" she seems to be. I help him inside the hotel and the elevator, using this as an excuse not to look at Melody. Mike is keeping her company enough by trying to achieve some kind of physical contact, but a quick goodbye in the elevator seals this very weird evening and as soon as we enter our room, Mike falls down on the sofa headfirst and mumbles into the pillow.

"What? I can't hear you," I say, slightly relieved to be in our suite and to have survived the night, although not all things turned out the way I wanted them to.

"I understand you now, Jack, there's something about Melody."

"Yeah, I noticed you trying to impress her with those lame jokes of yours. I hope I don't need to remind you she's getting married to my father."

"Damn, I wanted to be the third person I know who's slept with her," Mike jokes, "I don't get it though - getting married to your dad when she obviously has some kind of crush on you."

"Crush on me? I have no idea what she feels about me - hate, love, disgust. It's just crazy. And to add to that Cristina's father basically threatened me that if I ever hurt his daughter, you know?" I mimic cutting my throat.

"Ha-ha, he said that? He must've been joking, you and Cristina just met!"

"Yeah," I say and wish Mike a good night before I head to my room.

***

I can't sleep, because my head just won't shut up. All I'm thinking about is where I'm going with this, with Cristina, with my job, with my life, everything. Do I want to be an adventurous American in Mexico, pursuing the love of my life or do I want to be the old Jack Reynolds, roaming the night clubs in New York and putting in the extra hours to make yet another million? I'm pretty sure I'm tired of being the latter – but Mexico?

I'm just about to drowse off when I hear the familiar buzz from my Blackberry. A text message.

The display brightens up and tells me it's Melody. She wants to meet me somewhere and talk. It's four o'clock in the morning and I don't feel like getting out of bed, but I realize this had to happen sooner or later and it's actually good timing, since everybody else is asleep. So I push myself out of my gigantic hotel bed, put on some shorts and a t-shirt and head out to the beach at the back of the hotel.

I find Melody outside, dressed in pink shorts and a blue top, smoking a cigarette. She looks smaller than ever.

"Hi," she says, her voice cold as marble.

We walk down to the ocean without saying anything. The wind is quite chilly and I'm freezing, so I decide it's best to get this over with. I open fire first, because I firmly believe that attack is the best defense.

"So you're getting married, huh?"

Melody is stung, but prepared. "What do you care? I actually said yes to Hank two weeks ago. Before you came and fucked it all up."

"I fucked it up? I didn't think we fucked in any particular direction - we just fucked, meaning we both did. It was wrong, yes, but I wouldn't go as far as saying I'm solely responsible for it."

"You wanted me as soon as you laid your eyes on me, it was quite obvious, Jack."

"I'm a man, Mel, I was born obvious. And yeah, it was wrong, wanting you was very wrong, but you let it happen too. I mean you didn't have to kiss me or drive me to a super romantic place in the woods. Then none of this would have happened."

"So it's my fault now? You fucking asshole!" Melody spits the words out, but luckily not in my direction. She's firing up and needs to cool down.

"Take it easy, Mel, take it easy. We were both wrong. What's the point in finding the blame? It won't change anything."

"That's easy for you to say, you don't seem to have a tough time moving on. You wait a day and you find yourself a new girl. Is that how you play the game, Jack?"

"I know this looks like I'm the biggest douchebag to walk the planet, but believe me, this is a once in a lifetime thing, it's a crazy coincidence. I had to give up on us of course, it was the only thing to do and then I happened to meet Cristina."

"You never take any responsibility for your actions, do you? You just keep thinking about yourself and your own good. Couldn't you at least have told me you were leaving? I didn't know what happened to you and neither did Hank."

"I don't know what to say, except you were there too. You cheated on your future husband. I might have done a terrible thing, but you did one too. So don't try to shuffle all the blame on me. I take my part and you take yours. I don't even know why you're marrying my father to be honest. How long have you been living together, a few months? Sounds a bit premature to me?"

"Look at you then, you just met this Cristina girl and you're already making friends with the family? You have no right to tell me what to do and feel. Fuck you, Jack."

Melody sits down on the cold sand and starts crying. It's not a silent sob, but more of a panic cry, like she's hurt physically. I sit down next to her, but I don't know where to put my hand, on the leg, on the back? In the end I put it around her, but she shrugs it off. I have no real defense against crying women so I give in.

"Mel, Mel, please stop crying, we'll work this out. Things will be okay. Forget what I said, I know you love my father. You'll have a great life together."

We sit like this for a while. The sun is slowly coming up and we watch it together, my father's wife to be and I.

Melody's tears finally stop, but her face is still red and her cheeks swollen.

"Jack, I'm fucking confused. I'm marrying a man more than double my age - I love him, but you know, I still have second thoughts. I want kids. I want someone I can share my entire life with. With Hank, I know that's not very likely. Since I met you, the younger version of him, I've started thinking about these things a lot more. I'm always getting myself into things I cannot control and I'm so fucking tired of not being in control. My whole life I've been tossed and turned all over the place, always having to fight, never really getting the chance to make my own decisions. Maybe this is the same, maybe I don't want to get married."

"I understand you, believe me I do. I might not be the first to tell you, but I think you should call it off. Why the rush? Why can't you just take it easy and enjoy each other's company for now?" I put my arm around Melody again and this time she lets me keep it there.

"Hank wants it really badly. He would like to have a child with me, he said, even if we would have to adopt or something. He's so positive about everything it's like he doesn't see the fact he's 60 and he can't do the same things he did twenty years ago." Melody shrinks away right before my eyes. She's now the misunderstood child, wiping tears off of her face. Despite her screaming at me earlier, calling me an asshole, I feel sorry for her. It might be true the way she described it, she's been inside a human pinball game, thrown from one side to the other, never really stopping to figure out who she wants to be. In this case we're somewhat alike - we still have a lot of things to figure out.

"For a while I thought I loved you, Jack. We had been seeing each other for two days and I thought I loved you. How crazy is that? How can you love someone after two days? It seems like I was just running away from my upcoming marriage and you became my escape."

I don't really appreciate being called an escape, but I get what Melody's talking about. In some weird way we are connecting again, helping each other look inwards, like two mirrors - a bit broken, but still working, still reflecting. Maybe there's even a chance we could be friends.

"You know what? Nothing's lost. I'm not saying you have to break up with my father, there's absolutely no reason to if you love him. But you have to call off this wedding madness, because it's definitely happening too fast. If my father loves you the way he says he does, he'll understand. Instead I suggest you start thinking about where you want to be and think long and hard. That's what I'm trying to do, although it might not be going too well. Yet." I laugh and Melody finally smiles a little.

"Talking about happening too fast, how serious are you and Cristina?" Melody gives me a a concerned look.

"How serious can you be after a couple of days? I really like her though, that's all I know right now."

Then we just sit there silently for a while and look at the waves crashing into each other, exactly like we did, my friend and I.

***

When Mike wakes me up I'm surprised to find myself in my bed, because I have no recollection of ever getting there. But I do feel surprisingly good, considering the few hours of sleep I got, thanks to my talk with Melody.

Mike doesn't understand. "Why are you so tired? I thought you didn't drink last night?"

"I didn't go to bed until six in the morning. Melody sent me a text just after you fell asleep and we met outside for a walk and talk."

"A talk? How did it go?"

"It went pretty great. Got a ton off of my shoulders. Just a few more tons to go before I can feel normal again."

I give Mike the outline of our conversation, the wedding and her feelings about us.

"She's a nice girl," he says. "A bit lost, but a nice girl."

"You seemed to think she was a lot more than nice yesterday, good my father was too drunk to notice."

"Yeah, right," Mike says sarcastically. "I was just trying to be friendly."

"Friendly to her breasts," I say and walk out of my room where a big tray of coffee, orange juice, croissants and sandwiches are waiting for me. I instantly get the feeling that this can be the start of the best day in a long, long time.

***

Cristina and I are on Isla Mujeres outside Cancun, watching sea turtles. I'm not really that interested in animals in general (I was never a pet person), but Cristina thinks they're adorable and she really wanted us to come here. I must admit though that these huge creatures from the deep sea are spectacular and much preferred to the prehistoric human creatures of The Coral Gables Yacht club. It's a bit like watching dinosaurs come out straight from some forgotten era and interact with you.

We stand close by them now, Cristina all smiles and loving every minute of this. Myself, I'm loving every minute of her loving it. I stand behind her, kiss her on the neck and put my arms around her. It's really a blissful moment and I can't remember feeling so comfortable in my own skin before.

"They're amazing," I tell her. She doesn't notice that I'm looking at her breasts.

"Yes, they're so beautiful! You know Octavio Paz? The Mexican writer who won the Noble prize? He wrote something about the past worlds and how they follow us, watch over us, and judge us. These turtles remind me of that phrase because they're like guardians of time, you look in their eyes and see their soul, so old and wise."

Cristina says this with a sparkle in her eyes. She loves the arts, but although I prefer not to have poetry recited to me, I admire the passion in her, in fact I find it incredibly sexy.

Instead of talking literature, I kiss her. I'm a teenager again, I'm in love. Cristina giggles. She's also feeling it. I guess this is what happens to people in love, they get silly.

We're making out under the ageless eyes of the sea turtles and it's the most beautiful thing in the world. When we release, Cristina looks me in the eyes and says:

"Come with me to Mexico, come and stay with us, at least for a little while. See Mexico City. You'll love it, I promise."

I'm crazy about Cristina and she's probably the best thing that ever happened to me, but it's hard for me to love the idea of Mexico City and staying with Cristina's parents. I don't know how to say no though, because I desperately need to be around her to help me become my better self. So I say "why not?" and kiss her over and over again.

***

The following days are all about Cristina. I hardly even see Mike, Melody or my father, but I hear the three of them are hanging out a bit while I'm gone on my romantic adventures. When I know they're all out on another excursion, I sneak Cristina into our suite and we end up having a sweaty two-hour love session. It's like John Mayer sings – Cristina's body is indeed a "wonderland" and I would like to spend the rest of my days there if I could.

Despite being lost in the hazy fumes of love, I agree to go on a golf round with my father and Mike. We're nearing our leave date and I still haven't told Mike or my father that I'm going to Mexico City instead of New York City. So I hope the golf round will provide the excellent moment to announce it, since the focus will be on other things and hopefully lighten the mood. I know Mike must be pretty tired of being the fifth wheel and I feel for him, but I also hope he understands that, after all, love is what we're all really looking for.

My head's buzzing at the moment, but not with work as much as before, instead I'm slowly coming to terms with the feeling that I've done my last year at the firm. It's simply time to place my priorities elsewhere.

Why not move to Mexico? Learn Spanish? Write that marketing book I've been thinking about for years now. Maybe I could even start making furniture? Who knows? I would find something - that's for sure. Things will work out.

If I let them.

***

Golf - what an expensive waste of time it is. This is the first thought that enters my head as we step inside the clubhouse of the Cancun golf course Pok-ta-pok. As you know by now, I'm not really Sporty Spice, but I still picked up golf as my co-founding friend Nicholas sold it as an excellent way to conduct business deals. It was always a tough match for me though, because it's an extremely frustrating sport where a moment's lack of concentration can ruin a whole round. But my father loves the game's inherent and pointless quest for perfection and if I need a big chunk of his time, I'd better join him for a round.

Mike also likes golf. He even looks good in golf clothes, which is rare. But as I said, I'm not really here to play golf, I'm here to tell my father and my best friend that I'm following Cristina to Mexico City in a hopeful step towards a new life.

I'm pretty sure my father will think this is a good idea. After all the talk of settling down and procreation, he should be ecstatic. But with Mike I'm not so sure. I don't know if he dislikes Cristina or thinks I'm completely blinded by love. Maybe he just thinks it's bad timing, now that he needs my friendship the most.

It only takes a few holes to see that Mike's not really in the mood for golf. He's playing badly, sometimes hardly making contact with the ball and his level of frustration is increasing. I'm actually beating him at the moment, most of it thanks to some luck on my part.

"You're really playing well today, son." My father says in a cheerful tone, although he's far from happy with his own play. He's about to hit his third shot on the sixth hole and he's looking around his bag for the wedge, eyeing the rental clubs with suspicion.

Mike is to the right of us, his ball already on the green and he's talking into his phone. My father gives him a few annoyed looks, but I can hear on Mike's aggravated tone of voice that it's about work and there's nothing else to do besides taking the call. Poor Mike, reality seems to be hitting him hard. He still has to go back and face the single life in New York. If he's jealous, I can understand it.

My father hits his third shot only a foot or two from the flag and while Mike and I hit a good shot here and there, my father always seems to hit the ball cleanly. I'm starting to see how he finds such immense enjoyment in this - to be able to control the flight of such a small object while whacking the life out of it - must give him great sense of fulfillment. Although I really don't care about golf, I can't help but be impressed by my father's game - he's 60 years old and still has ambition, still looks for progress.

After the phone call it's apparent Mike's losing it. He curses after every other shot and when we're close to finishing the first nine holes, he hits the driver so hard the ball goes far out right and lands in the ocean. He mutters under his breath and takes another ball from his pocket, prepares his swing quickly and hits another shot just like it. He shouts "fucking shit!" and smacks the driver into the ground, likely bending the shaft. It's time I talk to him.

"Take it easy, man. It's just a game."

"Easy for you to say, you're playing fantastically, have a new girlfriend and everything's looking rosy."

"Rosy? I wouldn't say that, I'm happy I met Cristina of course. Should I take it you're not too happy for me?" I rarely see jealousy in Mike, so I'm a little surprised by his behavior.

"I'm happy for you, of course I'm happy - I'm just not sure I have anything to be happy about. I mean, where are you going with this girl? We're leaving in a few days – then what?"

My father's adjusting his stance, preparing his drive. He's muttering to himself, making ready. I don't know if this is the time to tell him, but I think to hell with it.

"I don't know, but I think for once I have to try going the full stretch. You said it yourself - I always pull away before I give myself the chance to actually feel something deeper. I'm trying hard to change that and I think Cristina might be the one to help me. So I have decided to go with her to Mexico, if only for a week or two."

My father drives the ball, slight hook, but still fairway. He turns to me. We've been talking through his shot preparation, but it didn't seem to bother him much.

"That's great news, son! Finally you're making a commitment," my father beams.

Mike isn't equally ecstatic. "So you're going to move to Mexico now? It seems quite drastic to me, especially since you said yourself you love New York and couldn't see yourself living anywhere else?"

"I'm not moving, I'm just going there for a visit, to feel it out - give it a proper chance."

Mike pretends not to hear this as he inspects his club. The head of it is slightly cracked, meaning one broken TV to me, and one broken golf club to him.

"I'm sorry man, but I just can't see anything good coming out of this. You think it's that easy to change your ways? What if you get bored with her like you do with all the other women you meet? What are you going to do then?"

I'm disappointed in Mike's negativity about my chances to actually have a real relationship. I understand him in a way, but it would give me more confidence to have my best friend believe in me.

"You're my best bud, Mike, and it hurts me that you feel this way. I'm really in love for once, but it doesn't mean things are written in stone, that I will move from New York, quit my job, change everything. I just need to go where my heart leads me."

Mike laughs in my face, "You should record yourself, Jack. You sound like you've started reading Paulo Coelho or something. I don't know if this is a part of your crisis, but it isn't you. The Jack I know doesn't say things like, I need to go where my heart leads me, that's for sure."

My father senses the hostility in the air and says: "Come on now, boys. Let's play some golf. Your turn, Jack."

A disturbing silence falls over us as I line up to hit the ball again. My good mood is gone. I'm feeling my sweat closely now, each drop running down my back. My pulse is roaring and I'm not seeing the ball properly. I try to follow my father's advice and look at the dimples on the ball, to concentrate on one of them, not the entire ball, but my anger doesn't allow me to focus. So I swing hard and in the middle of the motion, right where up is about to go down, something happens to my concentration and I hardly hit it at all. Instead of the ball taking flight, it bounces into the bushes.

I don't say anything, as there's nothing to say. I'm not going to start shouting at Mike in front of my father, I'm going to keep my calm and just play through the round for his sake.

But my father doesn't get through the round at all, because on the next hole, as he's walking over to the tee, he drops the club, moans and puts his hand to his chest. He sits down on his knees and I throw myself down by his side.

"Dad? Dad?" I shout as my world turns upside down again.

***

I have spent too much time in hospitals lately, first myself, and now my father.

"His blood pressure is very high and he was close to a heart attack," the doctor, a white-haired Brit with thick glasses and a helipad hairstyle, tells us. My father seems to be doing okay under the circumstances, but I'm not. Seeing my father on the hospital bed is a big blow, partly because I already lost my mother and didn't think there was a risk of being parentless at 35, but also because I couldn't think of a healthier 60-year-old man. He looks different now though, his constantly tanned face almost grey and lifeless. The only comfort I have is watching his chest heave slowly up and down, up and down. Melody is by his other side grabbing his hand hard and wiping her tears with the other. Mike sits in a chair behind me, and Cristina is on her way here. It's a strange support group, all shocked to see my father on a stretcher.

The doctor tells Melody that my father needs to eat better and stay away from fat foods. He also needs to take a few pills for a period of time. High blood pressure seems to run in the family and I can't help but think my collapse wasn't much of a coincidence. Hospital visits tend to remind us how fragile we are.

My father is allowed to leave the hospital later that night. He seems to be in good spirits, despite the shock, but he was of course always a stubborn optimist.

"This isn't the worst thing in the world you know, it's not like I was close to scoring my personal best or anything," he says and chuckles. The thought of results and progress is always there, even on a stretcher.

I'm impressed with Melody, who is the shining star through all this. She watches over my father's every step, makes sure he's okay, and holds his arm like it was about to break. I don't know if it's the love she hoped for, but it's some kind of love alright.

When we get back to the hotel my father says he wants to speak to me. Alone. So, as Melody leaves their room, I sit down next to him feeling the nasty flame of guilt burning inside me. It's so bad I consider telling him everything right now, admit to the affair with Melody, the lies, everything. But I guess it would only give him a real heart attack.

My father puts on his serious voice, "I know you're leaving for Mexico tomorrow and I just want to reiterate that this shouldn't stop you. Don't worry about me, I'll be fine. I know I've been on your ass for not settling down and it's because I want you to find the happiness I've experienced, at first with your mom, and now with Melody. You have worked so hard for your career and achieved a helluva lot and I think it's time you found someone to share it with. Cristina seems like that person, so don't let her go. I might get a real heart attack if you do." My father laughs at his own joke.

"I don't know what to say..." I stumble.

"You don't need to say anything, son. Despite my unexpected little incident I'm so glad we came. We've had a really good time."

"Yes, me too."

And then my father gives me a hug, a strong one and holds on for a while. It's the first real hug in, I don't know how long, and I can feel a little itch in my tear canal. It's like I finally got a bit closer to my father and that's great, but on the other side of me - the side where you'll find my damaged conscience - I realize I'll never be as close as I want to because of what happened with Melody, and that's what rips the feeling to pieces and leaves me hollow.

***

Mike and I are packing our bags when I realize that this trip has brought us closer together in one way, but further apart in another. Although I'm going to Mexico for only a week or so, it feels more definite somehow, like our friendship will never be the same again. That feeling makes me really sad, especially since it seems like now is the time when he needs me the most.

When our bags are ready we sit down on our presidential terrace for the last time.

"Mike?"

"Yeah?"

"I feel like shit."

"Why?"

"It feels like I'm leaving you. I know I'm not really, because I'm coming back to New York soon, but I just can't shake the feeling that I should've been a better friend, I should've been there for you more. But then I met Cristina..."

Mike interrupts me, "I appreciate that and don't worry, I'm an adult, life will go on and I'll be fine. Are you okay, by the way? You sound strange. I don't want to be mean but you sound a bit...all this emotional talk, it doesn't sound quite like you."

"I don't know, I'm having a bit of a rough time. I'm in love but at the same time extremely nervous about the trip and feeling massive waves of guilt for how I treat my friends, my father, pretty much everyone. I'm starting to worry I was born an asshole."

Mike gives me a sympathetic look, "Life's not easy and I know it hasn't been very easy on you lately - but remember this: you're not an asshole. You can be a bit of a prick sometimes, but the Jack I know is deep down a very nice guy." My best friend smiles at me.

I can't help but feel my eyes well up again. I've become an emotional wreck of late.

I fight the tears away and say, "Let's have a last beer to that," and then I head inside to the mini-bar.

"So," I say, carrying two bottles of ice cold Heineken, "what's your plan?"

"What do you mean? With Jo? Well, nothing. I can't say I'm over her, that will take longer, probably much longer, but I'm definitely through with her. Three years of my life wasted, just like that - takes some time to get over. I guess I at least learned something in the process and it's become a bit of a wake-up call for me." Mike takes a sip of beer and looks out at the ocean.

"What kind of wake-up call?"

"A reminder not to dream my life away, see things for what they are, and not be so goddamn blue-eyed all the time. You know, I thought I had it all, that this was how it was supposed to be. Man, I had no idea."

"Cheers to our wake-up calls then, Mike, one for you and one for me."

***

It's tough to say goodbye. It doesn't matter if you're going somewhere fantastic, to something you really look forward to. The hardest thing this time is that there's something final about it, because it's like we're all splitting up, taking different routes and starting new lives. I'm continuing my weird trip, following my nervous and awkward heart, trusting my instincts - despite concerns that they tend to lead me wrong. Mike goes back to work and a new life as a single man, an initially lonely life with lingering break-up blues. Who knows how he'll deal with it? Melody is staying in Cancun with my father, resting their hearts (and desires) and hopefully enjoying their no-must lifestyle. But is it what Melody really wants? Only she can figure that out. She has a heavy secret to bear and an upcoming marriage to a man with a weak heart. Does she have the heart to break it, if that's what she needs to do?

My father's already looking a bit more alive today, although I notice some melancholy in his eyes. I guess we didn't spend as much time together as we both wanted, but at least more than we've done in many years.

"Take it easy now, dad," I say and pat him on the back. I give Melody a long hug as well, because only I understand the burden she bears and that makes me feel a lot closer to her. I hope our weird little friendship can last.

Before I step inside the taxi to the airport, I shout to my partner in crime, "Mike! Prepare for some heavy drinking when I get back to New York. You're single now, life starts anew!"

And on that hopefully positive note, I wave goodbye to Coral Beach in Cancun.

***

Cancun Airport. I'm standing in line to board the plane, drinking a weak and almost transparent coffee from a plain paper cup. I'm not feeling too good, my nervous system strained around Cristina's family.

Cristina seems to pick up on this though and she chooses the right moment to hold my hand. This works temporarily, but I'm soon back to feeling stranded again, being the only American in the group. I only wish Cristina's family could have done a little more to make me feel comfortable, but Carmen and Salvador seem to have some kind of argument between them and they hardly speak at all, while Rico is occupied with his iPod. I know I have a big block of ice to break before we're all buddies and with Cristina's strong ties to her family, it's something I really need to focus on for this relationship to work. It would help of course if Christina's parents were a bit more down-to-earth, but wishing takes me nowhere - I just need to buckle up and deal with it.

As soon as we're airborne Cristina grabs my hand and holds it tight. She hates flying and leans her head on my shoulder like a child needing comfort from the imagined monster in the closet. I kiss her on the forehead and tell her it's nothing.

But I'm not sure I can tell nothing from something anymore.

***

My mood takes another dip when we touch ground in Mexico City. The sky is leaden and grey and the air thick and heavy like a winter coat. I step out of the plane, holding on to my cabin bag like it was my life vest in stormy seas.

Outside the terminal building I ask Cristina, "Is anyone coming to pick us up?"

"Yes, one of dad's drivers. You okay?"

"I'm fine. Just a bit tired, that's all." I smile at her, trying to keep the smile sincere, despite my impending sense of doom.

A big black van with tinted windows soon comes our way and Salvador waves casually to the driver. The car looks more like something for a famous politician than a man owning a furniture company, but on the other hand I don't know Mexico or the furniture business well enough. The driver, who's fat and wears a white shirt, black tie and dark sunglasses, says something in Spanish to Salvador and opens the doors of the van with the press of a button. We all climb in.

The murky mood stays with us in the car, it's almost like we're going to somebody's funeral. The air condition being on full blast doesn't exactly help to battle this morgue-on-wheels feeling. Driving from an airport never really offers you brilliant scenery, but together with the sullen mood and the dark skies, the grim and industrial surroundings give me a chill.

I put my hand on Cristina's leg in hope of feeling a bit better and she takes it, but her mind seems occupied. It seems like they've been arguing or talking about something sensitive and she doesn't want to tell me about it. So I sit quietly and look out the window, trying to find something positive in my head to cling on to.

After driving for some time both the sky and the city open up. Everything looks better in sunlight and together with the massive roads and views, I get a sense of how big this city really is, almost making New York feel small and cozy in comparison.

The van takes a left and drives through some pretty run-down neighborhoods and we soon get stuck in slow-moving traffic, giving me plenty of time to get a far too close look at poverty. Everything looks a bit broken here - the houses are in need of paint, the rusty balconies are filled with laundry and junk, and trash line the streets. It's not a pleasant sight. But I'm pretty sure the Gonzalez family lives in a more upscale neighborhood. They have to - they're obviously rich.

I don't need to worry long, because when the traffic clears, we reach a nice tree-lined boulevard and Cristina says we're closing in on the family house. The area, she informs me, is called Lomas de Chapultepec and according to her it's one of the nicest areas in Mexico City. My spirits lift among the green and I'm happy to see that most houses in the area look like mansions.

"Nice," I tell Cristina and she gives me a proud nod. We take a left turn and enter an arched and gated driveway. The driver picks up the remote again and at the click of a button the gate opens. I'm excited to see the house now and when I finally see it, I see dollar signs. It's basically a castle.

"Wow!" I exclaim and Salvador turns to me from the front of the car and says, "You like it, Jack?" and grins like a king.

In front of the white creation (which actually has a small castle-like tower as well) is a van and a large truck with "Mexmade" written on it, which I assume is the name of the furniture company that allows them to live in this kind of luxury.

"This is amazing," I tell Cristina, "I understand how there's room here to house the whole family."

"Yes, it's big, huh? Wait until you see the garden!"

When we're parked and everybody has gotten out of the car, two guys in white t-shirts and work pants come up and talk to Salvador. He mutters something and they open the back of the car and carry our bags up the long stairs to the front door. It looks like a well-rehearsed procedure and the Gonzalez family suddenly seems wealthier than I could've ever imagined.

"Who are those guys?" I whisper to Cristina.

"They are Mexmade employees, but right now they're here to work on my father's study. He works a lot from home and wants to have a really nice home office. My father likes to use his employees for all kinds of things around the house, he pays them well and expects maximum service and loyalty and I guess that's why people rarely leave us. Now let me show you the place."

The house is indeed one of a kind. What meets you when you walk through the door is a huge castle-like hall with stairs going up to a rectangular landing from where you can overlook the main room. When we walk around I get the feeling of being in a maze, with doors and rooms everywhere. You could easily get lost. The furniture is obviously made of wood and the pieces are classical and tasteful. The main room is huge and filled with marble statues, a large fireplace, and plenty of paintings with gold frames. I would have expected more color in a Mexican home, but here every wall is white, making a nice and modern contrast to the rich wood.

We walk up the stairs and Cristina leads me to a large bedroom with a bathroom and an en-suite shower.

"This is your room," she says.

"My room? We're not staying together?"

Cristina looks uncomfortable, "I don't think my parents would be too happy about that. They're firm Catholics. But I can sneak in here when they're asleep." She smiles deviously.

Then one of the workmen comes in behind us and puts down my luggage, which of course is only a carry-on bag. I don't get the time to say thanks before he scurries off. Cristina places a kiss on my cheek and says she's going to talk to her mom and leaves me alone with my bag.

When I unpack I'm instantly reminded I don't have any clothes. My luggage wasn't dimensioned for a multi-week trip and I'm running out of underwear, plus that Cristina must be tired of seeing me in the same shirts over and over again. I need to go shopping desperately.

I pick up my phone to find a message from my secretary, Angela. She wonders how I am and when I'll be back. Nicholas wants me to call him she adds, which I take as bad news. But work is thankfully so far from my mind right now, I can't really be bothered with it. I'm trying to feel comfortable in a stranger's home, in a new city, with a new woman and it requires my full focus. I have started writing my text back to her, when I feel a presence in the room. I turn around and find Salvador standing there and looking at me like he's waiting for me to say something. He scratches his arm and says:

"This was my dream, you know, to own a house like this. That's how it started. In my mind all successful businesses start from a dream. But you're a business man yourself so you know this already. What was your dream, Jack?"

Salvador's command of English is not bad, but his heavy accent forces me to really listen carefully. I'm desperate to make him like me.

"That's a good question, but I'm not sure I know the full answer. I remember growing up, wanting to have a really nice office," I laugh nervously, "and that's kind of how it started, I guess."

"And you have this office now?"

"Yes, I do. It's pretty much my dream office - I feel good being in there."

"You feel powerful in there." Salvador says, not so much a question.

"Yeah, I guess."

"A real man needs to feel powerful, it's important to us, it's what makes us work hard and fight for the things we believe in. The hunger for power might show itself in many ways, for example in a nice office, in a Ferrari, in a beautiful woman." I'm not sure where Salvador's going with this - I wasn't expecting some kind of speech.

"Do you still want power, Jack?"

"Yeah..."

"Because," Salvador interrupts, "I can give you power, money, the things you need to feel good. I can give them to you here, in Mexico City. You don't need to be in New York, you don't need to work for that company. Cristina told me you're tired of it, the business is not good anymore and you're often stressed. It doesn't need to be that hard, Jack."

Cristina already talked to her father about my issues? I don't like the sound of this, but I say "okay..."

"If you want to work with me, if you want to be a part of our family, you can get a lot more out of a job here. You can live in a nice house, drive luxury cars, and live a very good life. You can even have your dream office." Salvador chuckles.

"That sounds good." It's the only answer I can give him. I'm not sure how to deal with a talk like this so soon.

"I know this is early. We don't know each other yet. But my feeling about you stays and I think we can really be a great team. Think about it and we can talk when you're ready."

"I don't know what I would help you with though."

Salvador looks surprised by my uncertainty about his "offer".

"You're a modest man, Jack, maybe too modest sometimes for your own good. I have no problem finding use for someone with your skills. We have several outlets in Mexico, one in San Diego and we might be opening up more. And we could really use someone with your talent in advertising and public relations."

"Well, that's great. I guess I know a thing or two about those things, if that's what you're looking for."

"Tomorrow I will show it to you, our factory and office here in Mexico city." Salvador is obviously not used to get no for an answer.

"Sure," I say when Cristina's enters the room.

"Papa, does he really have to see that? I was thinking of taking him around the city tomorrow."

Salvador gives me resigned look, "Women. They always want to go to the city." He looks over at Cristina, "There's time for a city tour and an office tour in the same day, don't you worry my dear."

Salvador turns to leave, "There will be dinner in two hours, why don't you show Jack around?" He kisses Cristina on the forehead and leaves the room.

Cristina puts her arms around me, "Don't worry about my father. He's just so proud of the business, of what he's been able to create. He would really appreciate if he could show it to you."

"That's fine, it will be interesting." I say, still confused about being offered a job I'm pretty sure doesn't exist, by a man I don't really know.

"Want to take a walk in the garden?" Cristina looks at me with her puppy eyes and again I can't find anything else to say but yes.

We walk through the maze again, through the corridor and down the stairs, enter the big hall and then to the big adjacent kitchen where there are two maids chopping vegetables and boiling something in a couple of big pots. The smell reminds me I'm actually starving. Cristina tells me they're preparing tonight's big traditional dinner, with both relatives and friends coming. Carmen is overseeing the maids work in the kitchen and gives me a forced smile when she sees me. She doesn't seem very happy about my presence here, less so than Salvador, and I can't help but wonder what's behind it.

We walk through the kitchen and out on the back porch. The garden is like the house itself, gigantic. In the middle of the carefully cut bushes and trees, there's a majestic infinity pool giving the place a romantic vibe. We walk past it and find another Mexmade guy on his knees, digging in the dirt. He has a bag of seeds next to him so I guess he's planting something. Although he obviously sees us, he doesn't look up or say hi.

"That guy must be working pretty hard to keep all this in ship-shape," I tell Cristina as we're walking by some neatly cut hedges.

"Yes, but of course he's not alone working in a garden of this size. We want to keep it as nice as possible, because to us the green is important to the spirit. I walk through it every morning, to the back gate over there which leads to a small forest, where I usually go for a jog. It's my morning routine."

Behind the garden is like Cristina described, a thick and deep wooden area with a pathway made of wood and clay. Large trees soon surround us as we're walking uphill. Suddenly the air feels fresher, despite it being a really humid day.

"You've been really quiet ever since we left Cancun." Cristina looks at me, slightly concerned.

"I have? I don't know, I guess I'm a bit nervous about all this, being around your family, living with them. Your father is already talking about offering me a job."

"But you shouldn't be! My parents like you and my father must respect you a lot already to do something like that. He's obviously excited that I finally met someone."

"Yes, I'll try my best of course. It's just that I got a text message from work, my partner wants me to call him and they're pushing me to give a date when I'll be back. It's kind of stressing me out." This is a half-lie of course, the stress is not really work-related.

Cristina takes my hand to reinforce that she understands my concerns, but she really, really wants me to be here with her and forget about everything else. When I look at her, dressed casually in tight blue jeans and a yellow t-shirt, I almost have to pinch myself to believe this beautiful being wants to be with me. And that's how I need to see it - I'm lucky to be here.

The quiet of the woods makes me relax and helps me battle the small bouts of homesickness I'm feeling. I miss the city, my apartment, Starbucks, and my walks in Central Park. In a perfect world I could take Cristina there and we would live our life together in the city I love.

But this world is far from perfect.

I don't want to stay weird and quiet, so I ask Cristina what she thinks about during those walks and jogs in the woods.

"Stuff," she says, "sometimes I've had an argument with my mother, sometimes I think about love and sometimes about problems at work." I'm in a way happy to hear this - most of the girls I've dated before never gave the impression they used to think at all.

"So when you think about love, what do you think of then?" I know I'm treading haunted ground here, because I don't feel like hearing about ex-boyfriends or lost love.

"I don't know, I just hope I'll find love someday. Stuff like that. I guess I don't need to think about that anymore though," Cristina smiles. I smile back, because I'm happy there were no exes I need to hear about.

But she keeps on talking. "I never had many boyfriends. Of course, I've met guys, I'm not ten, but I've only had one long relationship. His name was Jorge. I was 16. My father hated him, because to him he was a gangster, lacked class and came from a poor family.

"Jorge was difficult, because he always seemed to go from one spot of trouble to another. I guess I kind of liked that then, thought it kind of exciting, but I also felt sorry for him and wanted to help."

"So what happened?" Not that I really want to know, but I feel obliged to ask. Why she is sharing this with me is not a hundred percent clear.

"It was terrible. He had an accident, a hit and run, and died immediately. They never found the person who did it." She looks sad thinking about it, but continues:

"That's kind of the reason I never met anyone I think, I was afraid and burned by that experience."

"I'm sorry to hear that", I say, genuinely sorry about Jorge's fate but at the same time glad to hear Cristina's relatively "untouched".

"What about you?" she says, immediately setting off the alarm button in my head. I really don't need to show off my reputation as a ladies man.

"I haven't had many relationships (true in a way), I haven't had the time." And then I smile and kiss her hard and then we lie down in the grass not far from her parents' house and make love.

***

It's time for the big dinner. The giant oak table in the middle of the dining hall is covered with plates and glasses and is set for what must be over thirty guests. Family is a big thing in Mexico and food is too. I wish I had a sports jacket and looked a bit more elegant, but my slightly wrinkled, white Armani shirt will have to do for tonight. Hopefully I can somehow charm the guests anyway, although it does sound like quite a tall task, considering my Spanish consists of about five words.

Cristina and I head into the lounge room where people are already drinking and chatting in loud and animated voices. This party doesn't need to break any ice, that's for sure. It's clearly one of those dinner parties where everyone knows everyone, everyone except me of course. I find it kind of strange to arrange a big dinner the same day you get back from a vacation, but maybe that's the tradition here.

I look over at Cristina with big eyes to show my surprise and she shrugs.

"Everybody's here to hear about the trip."

"Do they know about me then? Will this be very awkward?"

"I think my mother might have told some of them. Otherwise I'll just have to introduce you, I'm sure your looks will win them over." Cristina smiles, but let's face it, I'm a non-Spanish speaking American dating a family member, so there's no way this can be easy, no matter how attractive my face is.

Cristina isn't shy with showing our love though, she openly kisses me and holds my hand. She really glows tonight in a white linen dress and her hair done up beautifully in some kind of advanced knot.

"Let me introduce you," she says and takes my arm. My spine tightens up and I remind myself to relax and breathe deeply. The last few weeks have really shattered the image of alpha-male Jack Reynolds - now I'm just a scared little boy in love.

The first session of awkward introductions feels like visiting a retirement home, because I'm mostly saying hello to ancient people who don't know many words of English. I smile at them and they give me a tiny, uneasy grin back, like they can't really grasp what I'm doing there.

I'm not really sure either.

We walk around the room and in the corner we pass by a sofa containing two sharp-looking guys with greased-up and well-combed hair, wearing tailor-made grey suits. They look like they came straight out of the 50s. One of them has a tiny little mustache and slits for eyes. They eye me like I was a walking turd, which is pretty much what I feel like. The one with the mustache says something in Spanish to Cristina and gives me an annoyed glance. She responds heatedly and doesn't seem happy. I don't know how to react, but when Cristina looks at me and introduces me, I reach out my hand and they both shake it like they were shaking the hand of the devil. Then we walk out on the terrace. When we're out of hearsay, I whisper to Cristina:

"Who were those guys? They seemed to hate my guts."

"Don't worry about them, they're idiots. The one with the mustache is my father's younger brother Ricardo and Carlos is his closest friend. They both work in the family business, but with what, I'm not hundred percent sure. I think Ricardo supervises the San Diego store and travels a lot to the U.S. And if you wonder why they didn't seem to like you, it might have something to do with Carlos having a crush on me before."

I nod and think I might be even more unwanted here than I first thought. It wasn't going to be easy to cross the language barrier and cultural gap, but if there's bad blood already due to some other things...well then it will be very tough for me to stay with their family and in the future possibly live in Mexico.

I have nothing bad to say about the rest of the family though, they mostly seem kind, welcoming, although of course somewhat reserved. It might be a big thing for them to have a "gringo" in their house and I imagine them sizing me up, trying to figure out what makes me special, why their precious little girl chose me. Will I hurt her? Will I desert her? Do I deserve her? They don't know and frankly neither do I.

Cristina has wandered off to talk to her mother and I'm afraid that if I just stand here someone might come up and talk to me, so I head out into the garden where it's easier to "hide". I refill my wine glass on the way out and try to keep a friendly smile planted firmly on my face.

The garden is quiet, green and smells nice. I've been feeling tense all evening and here I manage to take a few really deep breaths and a little walk around the pool. I look into the water, almost expecting it to show me something, some kind of answer, because I'm starting to worry that there's no way I can fit into this style of living, with this big family, their alien language, culture and traditions. I really love Cristina, she's fantastic, but I don't know how high of a price I need to pay for her love.

As an answer to my question, I feel a hand on my shoulder and a voice from behind, "Baby, I was looking for you. It's time to eat."

***

The food is rich, massive, and strong. It hits your nostril like a boxer and lands in the bottom of your belly like a block of concrete. I know that with Mexican cuisine I might wake up at four in the morning and spend 30 sweaty minutes trying to give birth to Lucifer the turd, but it's too tasty and I'm also too hungry to resist.

The dining table is huge and I'm not happy to be placed in the middle, where everyone can look at me. The sound level that surrounds me can't be good for my ears and since I can't understand what they're saying or shouting, it becomes loud, aggressive noise. Cristina gives me a loving glance every now and then, but she's talking a lot to her white-haired table neighbor to the right, which leaves me without much of a conversation partner. I'm also unhappy to be placed opposite Ricardo and Carlos, who I imagine (because I'm trying not to look at them) are giving me hostile glances every now and then. Salvador is at the bottom of the table where most of the really old people sit, the grandmothers and grandfathers of the family, and Carmen is running around, talking to the kitchen staff and asking everyone, except for me it seems, if everything tastes good.

Most guests are finishing up their main courses and preparing for dessert (some of the guests have excused themselves to smoke or take a phone call) when Carlos suddenly opens fire. Just when I thought the mood at the table had shifted for the better and I was starting to feel a bit more comfortable, he pierces me with his eyes and says:

"Gringo!"

I almost jump up from my chair. There has been some pretty heavy drinking going on with margaritas, mescal and other local drinks being served in giant glasses and I've noticed Carlos being quite keen on the refills. I have no idea what he wants from me, but I'm pretty sure he doesn't want to just "shoot the breeze".

"Yes?" I say as politely as I can.

"You like Mexico?"

Carlos' English is decent, which I guess is a result of the Mexican-American empire of Mexmade.

"Very much I say. I haven't been here that long and seen so much yet, but so far I'm really enjoying it."

"You would really like to live here? In Mexico city?"

I don't know what to reply to that. If Salvador was hearing this conversation, which I doubt, because he's trying to shout something into the ear of one of the elders, he would expect me to say yes.

"Yes, I guess."

"You're not sure, huh? Of course, how can you be sure after only being here a short while? I must say it's quite gutsy of you, to come here, meet the family and everything, after only knowing Cristina a week. You don't even speak Spanish."

I'm starting to see where Carlos is going with this. He wants to make it clear to everyone that I don't belong here, with Cristina, in Mexico, at this table.

"Well, I was invited by the family and since I really like her, I thought it would be the right thing to do. I don't think there's anything strange about it. In regards to the language it's a shame I don't speak Spanish, I agree."

I look over at Cristina, but she's busy burning holes into Carlos with her eyes. The table is suddenly quiet and everybody seems to listen in on our conversation.

"You plan on learning it?"

But here Salvador comes to the rescue and says at the top of his voice, "Basta Carlos, basta!" which I take as meaning "enough", because the questioning stops.

After a few minutes, I go outside in the garden again, alone. Cristina is talking to some of her relatives and I don't feel like disturbing her, while I desperately need some fresh air after Carlos' attack. It has made me feel even more lonely and homesick, but also disappointed that even though I worked so hard to be polite, smiling and charming - I'm still despised. I'm too fragile right now to deal with it and it feels just typical of my recent luck that when I finally fall for someone, it seems impossible for all kinds of practical reasons to make it work.

The night is quite cool and I'm just standing there looking out into the garden feeling sorry for myself, when Cristina walks out.

"I'm sorry about Carlos, I didn't realize how big of an asshole he is."

"Why didn't you stop him then? It felt really bad to be questioned like that."

"I'm sorry, Jack. It's just that he scares me when he's in this mood. I hate how he made you feel and I'm ashamed for him." She reaches for my hand.

"I really hoped this would be easier, that's all."

"What do you mean, easier? This is just Carlos, he had a crush on me and he's a cabrón. Don't worry about him."

I know I should probably wait with what I'm about to say, but right now I feel strange and I'm not thinking properly - something which makes me open my mouth and let a big, black, slimy frog jump out of it.

"Couldn't you at least consider living in New York instead? I have enough money to support us both, you know that, and I'm sure you'll love it there. Your parents could come and visit us as often as they want."

Cristina unclasps her hand from mine.

"What? You already know you don't want to stay here? After one day with my family?" Cristina's eyes are throwing daggers, a side of her I haven't seen before, at least not directed towards me.

"No, no, don't get me wrong. I'm just asking why you don't come with me to New York for a few days, just to try it out. You said you wanted to go one day."

"One day is not now, is not living there. I want to live in Mexico, raise a family here and have my parents close. You know that! I can't believe you're talking like this!"

I realize I've opened a wound and I need to stitch it together right away.

"Cristina, baby, forget I said anything. You have to understand I'm a bit shell-shocked after that dinner. I just wanted to consider all the options."

Cristina looks unimpressed, "I want to live in Mexico, Jack. And I was under the impression you wanted to give it a real chance, that you would do anything to be with me."

Cristina's anger is fading out into sadness while I'm just sorry I started this New York discussion. I'm worried this whole me-living-in-Mexico arrangement is not going to work out, but I know it's too soon to tell and I need to give it more time.

Sadly, patience isn't one of my key skills.

***

The night stages a war between my stomach and the gas-friendly Mexican dinner. I'm twisting and turning and end up being thankful the bathroom is close by, because that's where I spend most of my time. Cristina doesn't visit me like we planned to and I guess I should be happy she doesn't. We're both a bit shook-up after the dinner and my stomach wouldn't do us any favors.

I wake early, but I'm feeling like a zombie and manage to fall asleep again. When I wake the second time, I find two messages in my Blackberry. One is from Mike and it reads: "Hola hombre, how's it going with the chica?"

I realize I haven't texted Mike (as I promised) about the progress or lack of progress, but then again, my mind has been elsewhere. The other message is from Nicholas. He rarely texts me nowadays, but I've been gone longer than communicated and I'm not surprised he's concerned. I text him that I need a few more days and then I'll be back in the office, refreshed and ready to go. I don't know if I'm complicating things by lying like this, because all I intend to do when I get back is resign.

There are sounds coming from the house. Glasses and cutlery are clinking in the distance, doors are opening and closing, the sound of footsteps penetrate the walls. The mansion is awake and has probably been for hours. While I shower I promise myself to try to start over and approach this day with a fresh and positive mind. Thanks in part to Carlos, it will be an uphill struggle.

The only person in the modern oak-tree kitchen is Cristina's brother Rico. He's dressed in light-blue Nike shorts and a white t-shirt with a Mexmade logo on it and wears the same drunken stare on his face as always. I assume he's another one of "dad's little helpers", because I couldn't even picture him flipping burgers at McDonalds. I bid him "good morning" as cheerfully as I possibly can and he gives me a nod back. You can't expect more conversation from Rico.

"Is there any coffee?" I ask him.

Rico points to the thermos on the counter. "Just take," he says.

The coffee is hot and strong, exactly how I like it, but with my nightly stomach battles, I'm not sure it's very good for me. I wonder where Cristina is, but Rico leaves before I get the chance to ask him. I hear a car start up on the driveway outside and I decide to head out on the front of the house to see if I can spot Cristina, but all I see is Rico driving off in a big Chrysler van. The air feels extra humid today, there's no breeze and together with the hot coffee, I'm starting to sweat. I sit down in one of the wooden chairs on the front porch and take a deep breath. The sun is already peeking through the trees and I'm not sure I'll be able to sit out here very long before I need to take another shower. But I'm enjoying this, a calm and quiet moment outside with a cup of morning coffee, it's life in its most glorious simplicity.

The moment of calm and quiet doesn't last long though, because I suddenly see someone coming towards the house in a turquoise training top and black leggings. It's Cristina.

"Morning hunny," she shouts, running up from the driveway, panting slightly.

"Morning beautiful. You're out jogging already?"

"Si, I thought of asking you, but you needed the sleep." She runs up the stairs with a spring in her step and kisses me on the cheek.

"You slept well?"

"It was a bit up and down to say the least." I rub my stomach to indicate why.

"Not used to comida Mexicana, eh?" Cristina laughs.

I feel a fart come on, but I suppress it and force a smile instead.

"I talked to my father. He wants to take you on that tour if that's okay with you?"

"Yes, sure," I say although that's exactly what I don't want to do right now.

***

Salvador's a different man today. Yesterday he was reserved - today he's boastful. He's showing me his life work, so I guess he's right to be. His dress code is serious with a nice dark suit, a white crisp shirt and burgundy-colored tie.

"You look nice." I nod towards his getup.

"Gracias. You ready? Let's go."

Salvador goes up to Cristina and kisses her on the forehead like the "godfather" he is.

"Don't let him bore you to death," Cristina says, as Salvador is gesturing towards the black Mercedes on the driveway.

"Oh, he won't." I tell her and think that if I ever die at the hands of Salvador, it wouldn't be through boredom. Then I wave goodbye.

I thought Salvador would be at the wheel on a casual drive like this, but he's not. We have another driver now, a big man in a suit and sunglasses. He doesn't seem to acknowledge my presence.

We both sit down in the back of the car. Salvador says something to the driver and off we go.

Salvador must sense what I'm thinking and says:

"Jack, having a bodyguard might seem strange to you, it's maybe not the world you come from. But let me explain. I'm a successful businessman living in the biggest city in the world, a city that from time to time can be very dangerous. This makes me a target and that's why I have some protection. Most wealthy people here do."

Bodyguard? I thought the big guy at the wheel was a driver. Is this the kind of lifestyle they want me to adapt to, a life where you can't leave the house without "protection"?

Salvador goes on, "It's nothing to be nervous about, it's just something I want my family to have. It means I take care of them."

"So these guys," I nod towards the driver, "follow you everywhere?" I say anxiously.

"Usually I have at least one of the guys go with us, but for our vacation, our anniversary, we said we would go only family. Cancun is not the same as Mexico City."

I've heard Mexico City is a dangerous city, I thought maybe on par with New York (which feels quite safe to me, thank you very much, Mr. Giuliani), but now I understand that this is on a completely different level. I also understand why Cristina never told me this, because it wouldn't be good advertising for the city she wants me to live in.

Salvador suddenly changes the subject.

"You know, Jack, for three generations our family has worked hard to create the most beautiful handmade Mexican furniture. In fact, my great grandfather created many of the pieces in our house himself. He worked in his garage with simple materials and tools. Word spread about his great craftsmanship and relatives, friends and later also complete strangers, wanted to own this kind of furniture. So he opened a small business and started making some money. Not big money, but enough to grow a little bit every year. We were doing well even when my father was alive, but after his death I decided to start exporting across the border. This is what changed it all for us. We took on an international name and now we make very good money, have a shop in San Diego and several around Mexico."

"That's great," I say, trying to sound enthusiastic, "what a nice story," but I'm still wondering what kind of danger I'm in, riding in a car with Salvador and his bodyguard.

Salvador looks at me and smiles. "Wait until you see the factory."

There's quite a distance between the Gonzalez mansion and the Mexmade factory and we need to travel through some pretty shady-looking areas to get there. As I look out the tinted window, every fiber of my body wishes it was in New York. It's a bit heartbreaking really, because I can't help but feel how difficult it will be for me to live here, even though I owe it to Cristina to try. I guess my long-term hope is convincing her we can live in New York, but right now I don't like my odds.

After driving through another grey and worn industrial area we stop in front of two big metal gates with a large sign saying Mexmade. The logo looks a bit out of place for a factory, it's more like something you'd find on a juice box, with swirl in orange and the text in a mix of orange and blue. But I guess that's just the ad man in me thinking.

We drive onto a large driveway with at least five or six Mexmade vans parked there. As we exit the car, I wonder briefly what kind of relationship you have with a bodyguard. Are you friends? Do you have dinner together? Or is it strictly business - the business of life and hopefully not death?

The driver/bodyguard slowly puts the car to a stop, opens the door, climbs out and brushes a few crumbs off of his suit jacket. Then he picks up a cigarette and lights it. I don't think he has any interest in the tour, he's just here to protect us. From what I can only imagine.

Salvador walks to a small aluminum door next to the huge garage-style one and waves me over. He puts the key in the lock, fiddles a bit with it and then opens the door. "Welcome to Mexmade", he says as we step inside darkness. He walks a few steps to the left and pulls a switch which makes a clunk sound. Lights are switching on one by one and the huge workspace opens up before my eyes. The place is massive with big, brand new machines and blue-white number signs hanging from the ceiling, likely indicating different workstations. My nostrils are awakened by a strong and not too unpleasant smell of sawdust.

"Atchoo!" I sneeze.

"Ahh...wood and also dust," Salvador chuckles. "Let's take a look around."

The place is completely empty of course, as we're here on a Saturday. Salvador tells me about the different kinds of wood they're working with and his love for the material, while I'm lost in my own thoughts. I was never a handy person and I don't really care much about wood, but my ears perk up when he says there are a lot of rich people in places like LA and San Diego buying Mexmade furniture. Somehow I couldn't have guessed it.

"The craft runs deep in this family, wood for us is love, passion, life. It's a living thing and you have to treat it as such." He holds up a plank and caresses it like a woman.

He asks me if I can wield a hammer or saw.

I don't want to disappoint, but I can't lie either and say, "I'm not really that much of a handyman."

This nets me a discouraged grunt and "of course you're an office person, a word person." He knows I work in advertising, but we've never really talked about what I do, which is weird, because he has practically offered me a job.

After a tour of "the floor" we walk upstairs to the offices. Salvador's office has big windows overlooking the work floor and it's high up enough to give a decent view of the surrounding area as well. The office also holds a really massive mahogany desk with pictures of his family scattered around it. I don't see any computers anywhere, which surprises me. When I ask him about it, he says he doesn't trust them. Being a paper person, I know what he's saying.

We have a coffee from the machine near the kitchen and walk outside.

"I think you're a good man, Jack. You have guts. Because it does take guts to follow a girl to a new country and meet her family after knowing her only a short while. I take it your love for Cristina must be very strong and I really appreciate that." He looks straight into my eyes, giving me a serious look.

"I must say I was a bit skeptical about all this at first, but on the other hand I've never seen Cristina happier and I trust her heart more than anything, because she really has a beautiful heart. And if my daughter loves you, then you're family to me. I hope you feel that."

He grabs my shoulder and squeezes it hard.

I don't know what Cristina has told him, but it seems like he's under the impression that my move to Mexico is already decided.

If he only knew the doubts in my head.

***

Cristina is waiting outside when we get back home and I'm so happy to see her I could cry. In my current fragile state tears never seem far away. I'm torn between the loveliest woman I've ever met and living in a country I don't think I can ever live in. Not that there's something wrong with Mexico, it's just the Gonzalez version of Mexico I don't feel very good about.

Cristina is going inside to collect the car keys for our upcoming trip to the city and after a little while I hear her voice and then Salvador's. It's not normal conversation, not even for heated Mexicans. They're definitely arguing about something and it makes my stomach tighten.

After a while Cristina runs out and I can see she's furious. She points to the black BMW parked next to me. We sit down in it and she slams the door shut.

"What's wrong?" I ask her.

"It's my stupid father. He always wants security around me - he's becoming completely paranoid. I mean, I grew up in this city and I'm an adult now, I know the risks. Just because he has a lot of money he thinks everybody's out to get him."

"So what happened?"

"I'm not listening to him for once, we're going alone." Cristina turns the key, reverses with a jolt and takes us out of the driveway.

During the first kilometer she's grabbing the steering wheel hard, her hands almost making an imprint in the leather and her eyes black from anger. We're both silent. I can see she's trying to come to terms with their argument or possibly something else, while I feel completely numb, watching her hurt while my head's spinning like some broken doll. Then, as the signs seem to be leading us towards the city center, she starts crying, her anger slowly seeping out of her.

"What's wrong?" I ask her, but I think I know.

"It's...it's just that sometimes I get very angry with my father. I guess it comes as no surprise to you that he tries to control my life. He always has. I know it's out of love, so I let him do it most of the time, but sometimes it just feels so stupid."

"I guess that's normal though, your father wants what's best for you and what you're feeling isn't strange at all."

"Maybe, but my father can be very tough, controlling and demanding. It's his way or the highway. I'm really thankful he's taken to you, otherwise this wouldn't have been easy."

This doesn't come as any surprise to me of course, Salvador could scare the daylights out of the real life Marlon Brando.

"In what way is he controlling you?"

"I can't really explain. He doesn't do it like you would think - he's not violent or dominant. He just says these small things, sometimes making me feel bad for the choices I make on my own."

I regret the need to start this whole thing up again, but the opportunity is too good not to.

"Wouldn't it be a good idea to live away from him then? Not let your relationship get so strained?" I know I might be nagging her, but I can't help it. This might be the only way. Her life here is so different from how I imagined it back in Cancun, when my eyes were colored by romance.

"Jack, please, I can't think about moving right now. You're asking too much."

My heart sinks when I realize that all along I might really have been asking too much.

***

The best shopping area of Mexico City is bustling. It's like an animal alive and I wish I was ready for it. But I can't relax and take it in, instead I feel like crying. I just don't know what to do about all the mixed feelings I'm having.

I experience a big deja vu when I walk through another massive department store with Cristina. It makes me think of Melody and that I was doing exactly this in Coral Gables with her not long ago. It's a weird feeling which leads me to my father and suffocating guilt. I had hoped these feelings would fade slightly, but now they rise to the surface, bitch-slap me and leave me breathless.

I need to buy clothes though and try to focus on that. Jeans and shirts, jeans and shirts. Anything will do, because I'm too emotionally exhausted to be in a cramped changing room.

I'm again reminded of my homesickness by the street Presidente Masaryk. There's some small part of New York here, although the streets aren't as wide and the buildings not as high and of course I don't feel close to what I do when I'm in New York. New York is home and this is not and it's becoming far too obvious to me.

After a few hours in the nice super-brand stores in the Polanco area, we sit down at a fancy roadside café. I order a dish I can't pronounce and a beer, knowing I will probably need more than one to subdue my demons.

Cristina orders a glass of white wine in that beautiful Spanish accent of hers and looks very relaxed. She has no idea what I'm feeling and in this case, it's probably for the better.

"It's not so bad this city, right?" she says and I can tell how happy she is to be here, how home this is to her.

"It's nice. It ain't New York, but it's nice."

Now why do I say a thing like that? What makes my brain shit out words which were meant to exist only in my head? Have I started to drift completely? Drift away from the city, the situation, her. It's a weird feeling, but I've had it many times before, in other relationships and situations. It's the familiar feeling that when the going gets tough - Jack gets going.

Cristina looks like she just can't believe I said that and her mouth tightens to a thin line. A garbage truck passes by and the smell vividly illustrates the mood.

"You Americans never appreciate anything un-American, it's so typical." And here it comes, the anti-Americanism I had hoped was absent in Cristina, but is now flying out of her. I usually welcome her saliva, but now I dodge it like a bullet.

"Don't get me wrong Cristina. I'm really enjoying myself here, I was just trying to sell New York to you." I give her a shrug and a smile. That's the best I can do, although I'm probably looking and sounding like a cabrón.

"Yeah, that's what you do, you sell things," she says with quite a bit of venom. I make up my mind to bite the bullet.

"I do. I want to sell a life in New York. I want us to have a life in New York."

"Are you stupid or what? I told you we can't! Why aren't you listening to me? I have a life here! My whole family is here! What do you have back in New York? A friend and a job you hate?"

Cristina the ice queen is slowly melting and I can see her tear ducts starting to work. I'm very sorry I hurt her, myself, everyone.

"I came here to be with you, to experience Mexico City, to meet your family and learn more about you. We've only been seeing each other for two weeks. I guess what we need is time."

But Cristina is already keen on piercing my defenses: "I thought you were quite sure about this move, back in Cancun you were talking about a new step in your life, a welcome change. What was all that talk about then? Just to get me into bed?"

"No, of course not! I just want the best thing for us. I really, really like you and I think we can be very happy together, but it will be difficult to live with bodyguards, your skeptical family and my lack of Spanish. I just felt it would be so much easier in New York."

I'm not sure if Cristina is about to cry or splash her wine glass in my face.

"So now you won't even consider living here? Is that what you're saying, Jack? Is this place so bad? Is my family so horrible?"

Here all my sales skills, all my acquired talent for communication and tricky social situations, is worth nothing. I need to beg like a naughty child, I need to humiliate myself to salvage the situation. So I kneel down beside her and whisper: "Of course it's not horrible here. I'm happy anywhere as long as I'm around you. I'm just feeling a bit homesick that's all. It was stupid of me and I'm sorry." I try to put my arm around her, but of course she waves it away. She gives me a look of resignation.

"Jack, I can't leave my family and I don't want to have this discussion anymore. If you can't consider moving here, then you're not the right person for me."

And to that I have nothing to say. Not yet. Not now.

***

When we leave the café we're both exhausted. I've tried to assure her that what just happened was a temporary glitch in my behavior, but of course she doesn't seem very convinced by this and neither am I. The only thing I know right now is that I can't take any more of her crying, so I'll try to keep my stupid mouth shut.

Cristina looks to the right of her and mutters something angry in Spanish and, as to translate for me, she adds: "I can't believe this."

"What? What is it?"

"I can't believe he did it, mierda! I can't believe this shit. You see the black Mercedes over there? That's one of my fathers' cars. They're following us."

"What? Are you sure? Why?"

"If he can't get me to accept security, he'll make sure I get it anyway. That's how my father works - he doesn't take no for an answer. Come!"

We walk swiftly from the café with Cristina looking over her shoulder every other second. We're followed and we're running away, and if that's not fucked up, I don't know what is. We see the black car starting up behind us and we disappear across the street and into a nearby department store, take the elevator, go to the second floor, exit onto another crowded street then half-run down it. Finally, we reach a nice park where we, panting and out of breath, sit down on a bench. I look over at Cristina and she's smiling.

"Think we lost them?" I say.

"I think so. Pretty exciting life, huh?" Cristina throws her arms around me and kisses me and to my surprise, I feel a wave of happiness, which feels strange and out of place considering everything that's been going on. Maybe the run released some of our pent-up stress.

We buy ice cream from a candy stand and sit down in the sun. I'm feeling my heart rate slow down and I'm finally relaxing a bit. The park was exactly what I needed to find calm and Cristina seems happy again too.

In a spark of inspiration, I tell her I'll reconsider Mexico City, that I will enjoy these next few days and that the most important thing right now is that we stay together. I'm suddenly feeling much better and I'm seeing possibilities again - the book I wanted to write, the new stress-free lifestyle I wanted to lead, it can all be here, with her. I just need to open my mind a teeny bit more.

We spend an hour in the park, just talking, kissing and laughing out all the previous tension. While the sun is warming my face, I look at her and realize I could spend the rest of my life just watching her beautiful face with her perfect skin, golden and glowing. I have already picked up on her cute little mannerisms, how she squeezes her lips together sometimes when she's thinking and the way she fiddles with the locks in her hair when she's nervous. I also love her voice, which is low and soothing most of time, but more raw and passionate when she gets excited and I love her accent which makes it all come alive in a wonderfully exotic package. I can go on and on about her, make this paragraph into a romance novel and although I know I might not really be fit to love, if there's one person worth all my efforts - it's her.

***

In the car on the way back to the mansion, I text my father. He texts back quite fast, telling me he's out on his first golf round after the "incident" and that he's hitting the ball like Tiger Woods. He asks me how I am and writes he's been thinking a lot about me. Maybe it's the heart attack who has made him reconsider things the way I have lately. No matter what it is, it's a change I think we both welcome.

Cristina is at the wheel, throwing looks in the rear-view mirror to make sure we're not being followed, but she doesn't look worried - she looks confident and happy.

I suddenly realize what I need to do.

"Baby," I say.

"Yes?"

"I think I need to go home, sort out work and a few other things and then come back here."

"Now you mean?"

"Well, the sooner I leave, the sooner I can come back. I realize I need to untie some strings back home to be here in full and give you everything I can. Now I'm constantly stressed about work and the lack of stuff I have with me. If I can sort out my work situation, we could rent an apartment here and properly try it out! I could write the book I've been thinking about and you could keep working at Mexmade, but without having to stay with your parents. It would be a new life!" Suddenly I'm excited like a little boy.

"It sounds great. I just don't want you to leave." Cristina does the puppy voice again.

"But I'll come back soon, I promise. I'll call you every day!"

But Cristina can't hide her disappointment and her fears, "Are you breaking up with me, Jack?" Her voice cracks and she looks into my eyes.

"Of course not! I love you! This is not a break-up, it's a revelation!"

"I just need you to be honest with me. It would be so easy for you just to go home and forget about me. I know how guys are." She's exactly right. That's how I act. Usually.

But this is not the old Jack talking, this is Jack 2.0 and he's speaking the truth! I reach over and kiss her again and whisper that I love her, hoping I can convince her the same way I've managed to convince myself that this is what's right and true.

***

Coming back to New York is always something I look forward to - something deep within my bones, but on the way back to my penthouse I don't even have the energy to engage in the friendly or sometimes unfriendly banter with the taxi driver. Instead all I can think about is Cristina. I miss her so much it hurts.

It's a pretty warm night in New York City and the apartment smells fresh, because my cleaning lady was there during the day. I put my bags on the floor and walk into the kitchen, open the nearly empty fridge, grab a bottle of Budweiser and take a long, refreshing sip. It feels really strange to be back in my bachelor pad. It feels lonely.

I know I'm in desperate need of a shower, but first I need to call Mike.

Mike doesn't pick up until the sixth ring. He's out of breath and panting loudly.

"Jack!"

"Hi Mike."

More panting. Have I called a hotline?

"What are you doing over there, Mike? Are you fucking or something?"

Suddenly Mike comes to life: "Ugghh, no, no. I was just riding my exercise bike."

"You have an exercise bike? Since when?"

"Well, I bought one. You know I need to get in shape. Where are you? Still in Mexico?"

"No, I'm in New York. It's a long story and I wouldn't mind sharing it with you. Is it okay if I come over?"

"You mean now?"

"I need a shower first, but after that, yeah."

"Okay, that should be fine."

"See you soon then, compadre."

And we say goodbye.

When I step inside the shower, I can't help but feel like a stranger in my own home. I don't want to be here, I want to be where Cristina is. Wherever she is.

And I also need to know who Mike's been fucking. Exercise bike? My ass.

***

Mike's place post-Joanne is a hellhole. I never actually liked his West Side one-bedroom apartment, it's dark and not particularly homely, but now Mike has also filled it with so much crap I almost step back into the corridor when I see what he's done to the place. Mike used to be quite tidy, definitely more so than his ex-girlfriend Joanne, but single life must have really deteriorated his sense of order. I walk past two pairs of jeans lying on the floor and enter the kitchen, where there are empty cereal boxes stacked on the kitchen table and a mountain of dirty dishes in the sink. I open one of the cupboards and the only clean beverage container I find is a mug with a HP-logo on it. I take a half-empty bottle of Famous Grouse from the cabinet and sit down on the only chair with nothing on it and pour myself a drink. Mike is ironing shirts in his underwear while watching Bloomberg TV. A very "serious" channel for a bum, I would say.

"You sure need a girlfriend, Mike. Or why don't you at least get a cleaning lady? I mean sanitation crew." I look around the room in disgust.

"It's a dump, I know. But I haven't had the time. Work has been crazy ever since I came back from Cancun. Besides, I've started going to the gym." Mike grins and flexes an unimpressive bicep.

"Nice to hear. You do look a bit slimmer."

"So tell me, how was it?"

"It was awkward and fantastic at the same time. Her family sure is weird, but I really, really like her. I still feel like she's the one for me." I can't help but feel a buzz inside of me when I say these words. Finally, things might be falling into place.

"Wow, I thought maybe things didn't work out since you're back already. But you really have a crush on her, don't you?"

"You bet your fat ass I do. She's amazing."

Mike wears a concerned look on his face, "So what's going to happen? Are you going to move there?"

"I think so. At least to try it out. The plan is to rent an apartment together and take it day by day."

"Oh." Now it's Mike's turn to wear the sad puppy look.

"I know it's not ideal from a friendship point-of-view, but I really need to do this, I really need to take it all the way. If I give up now, I'll hate myself forever."

"I understand. It's just a shame that it has to be in Mexico that's all. But I'm of course also happy for you. Jack Reynolds, settling down - who would have thought?" Mike has a wry smile on his face.

"Yeah, who would have thought? But hold your horses for now, it's a test."

"So you're finally quitting the agency?"

"Yeah, it's time to push the boulder from my shoulder. I'm going in tomorrow. I have a lunch booked with Nicholas and then we'll take it from there."

"Wow." Mike says and pours himself another glass of whisky.

"Yeah, lots of changes happening." I say and drink from mine.

"You know what?" Mike says, "Let's go out. We won't have many other chances, so let's make it a night to remember."

"Okay," I say, but I'll do it for Mike's sake, because I'm not really in the mood.

***

The New York nightlife used to be my second home. I was happy and comfortable to roam the clubs like a rock star and pick up girls at will. Tonight I'm no rock star though, I'm a dinosaur and the line to my friend Gino's trendy nightclub confirms that. The only good thing about being a dinosaur is that you've been around long enough to skip it.

I skim the line-up as I walk by it. Most of the girls are attractive, but way too young, way too slutty and way too not-Cristina.

Back in my "glory days" I could pick up one of these girls in the blink of an eye, tell them to come with me, Mr. VIP, drinks are waiting. It was confidence and power mixed with some kind of desperation. And the sick thing was that I wouldn't be surprised to see them leave their boyfriend standing there for a slim chance with someone who they didn't know, but who somehow promised a more glamorous existence.

But that feels like a lifetime away. These days I don't even know if I could muster the courage to talk to them, not that I want to either, because now I have Cristina.

Mike is ready to party though - I've rarely seen him so anxious to drink. I don't mind it, especially if it could help him get all those Jo-tainted brain cells erased. Then it's for his own good. And mine.

Props to Gino who has really taken the place up a notch. He's replaced the lounge furniture, put up some pretty expensive chandeliers and really worked hard on the lighting. Besides, he knows his marketing - he understands that if he pays celebrities to show up every now and then, the popularity of the place will soar. I wouldn't be surprised if this is now one of the hottest clubs in New York and I'm happy for Gino, who I got to know a few years ago when I was going through my perhaps craziest party period and didn't sleep many hours per night. Gino is half-Italian and looks the part, meaning there's always a girl or two by his side. This time he shows up with a young Restylane-lipped blonde as his girlfriend of the night. Or the week.

"Jack, my friend, such a long time! Where have you been?"

"Hi Gino! Work, travel, holiday, to summarize. What about you, everything good?"

"Very good, in fact. We had Lady Gaga here on Saturday - can you believe that? She's a wreck though. Man, I would worry if I were her father. By the way, my brother was just asking about you, we should have dinner, catch up."

I don't know how many times I've heard this dinner proposal, but it has never materialized. It's taken me a while to come to terms with the fact that the friends you have during the night, are not the same in the daytime.

Gino walks away but soon returns with two of his special Gino Mojito's – a spicier version of the popular Cuban cocktail. I don't know what kind of extra ingredients he puts in there, Tabasco is likely one of them, but they do kick-start your night in a tasty way.

This is strangely enough the first time Gino meets Mike and I don't think they're the best match. Mike is not really the right type for this place, which you can judge by his tucked-in blue shirt and khaki chinos. He looks like a dad on a Sunday lunch with the family, not a guy ready to buy bottles of champagne for a table full of hot girls, which is the usual procedure here. Gino, who's very fashion-sensitive, looks Mike up and down. He's probably trying to figure out why I invited Mrs. Doubtfire to the party.

Mike doesn't sense any of this, as he's busy taking huge gulps of his Gino Mojito. His primary focus right now is drinking, not fashion.

Gino leads us to one of the VIP lounges where we have a private table waiting for us with a nice view of the dance floor. I'm starting to relax a little bit, but it's not the alcohol so much as the familiar surroundings. After being on the emotional roller coaster ride I've been on, it's nice to feel at home somewhere – even if it's in a nightclub.

Mike quickly finishes his drink and asks the waitress for shooters and beers. The train is in motion.

After a while Gino comes by again, trailed by two young girls. For some reason I pay more attention to Gino's shirt than to the girls. It's white, crisp, with semi-thin purple lines and it makes his oversized Breitling watch stand out like a trophy.

"Gentlemen, this is Tara and Britney," Gino smiles his nightclub owner smile. He turns to the girls: "Girls, this is Jack, (he points his finger at me) one of the leaders in advertising today and his friend...Mike."

The girls say hi, almost in unison. Mike usually freezes around women, especially attractive ones, but he's already softened enough by the drink to overcome a part of his social tentativeness. The ladies sit down and Gino leaves, maybe to find his neglected date, if he hasn't already forgotten about her.

I would usually take charge here, order drinks, turn on the charm, but instead I'm suddenly awkward, uninterested and distant. The only thing that keeps popping into my head is the image of Cristina, in my arms, looking out on the sea. It's an image I want to be in, not only think about.

I wake up enough to tell Mike to get the ladies some drinks, but as soon as he's left the table I realize my mistake, as I have no idea what to talk to them about. I throw out some empty questions, but although the girls answer them enthusiastically, I'm completely uninterested in their replies and we're soon all turning our heads uncomfortably to look for Mike and the drinks. I sigh to myself and think that my mojo must finally be dead. I'm about to excuse myself to go to the bathroom when Mike comes rushing, red in the face and eyes big and scared. "We need to leave," he says, directed only to me, not the girls. He's breathing heavily.

"Why? What happened?"

"I think I just broke a guy's nose. They've called the police. We have to go."

Mike's expression tells me this is no joke. I excuse myself for a second while the girls just stay where they are, shocked. Mike and I are heading towards the exit when Gino comes our way, looking pretty pissed off.

"What the fuck is this about, Jack?" He doesn't even look at Mike. "You can't bring this kind of people here. I don't want any fights in my club."

"I'm really sorry, Gino. Mike, what the hell happened over there?"

Gino doesn't let Mike reply.

"I can tell you what happened. Your friend went up to a guy at the bar and hit him in the face. Hard too. Knocked him over. The guy is over there on the floor now, bleeding from his nose."

I don't know how to react to this, besides getting our asses away from the crossfire.

"Okay, I understand. Can you please tell the guy to calm down and we'll leave right away. I'm sorry, Gino."

"I think you actually know the guy, I've even seen him here with you if I'm not mistaken."

"What?"

Mike steps in, his voice low. "It was that guy, Russell I think his name is. He was here with Joanne. He's the one she's been sleeping with and that's why I freaked out."

"Russell? My friend Russell? He's sleeping with Joanne?" I'm dazed and confused, but Gino is still alert.

"Guys, guys, I need you out of my club. I'll take care of this, don't worry, but I don't need anymore shit like this in my place, okay?"

"Okay, okay, thanks Gino," I say and we head out into the lukewarm New York night. We're walking fast uptown, heads down like we're getting away from a crime scene. I wouldn't call it a crime to hit a guy in the face, at least when he's slept with your girlfriend, but Mike seems to be completely in shock about the whole thing. He hasn't said a word since we left and he's basically shaking with anger.

"Mike? Talk to me, Mike."

"I can't believe I did that. I just can't believe it." Mike's voice breaks, "What's happening to me?"

"Nothing is happening to you. You did what most guys would do, you stood up for yourself."

"When I saw Jo I was fine, no anger, no nothing. I just slept with the girl, you know. I thought of going up to say hi, but as I was approaching her, this suave asshole came up behind her, put his hand on her shoulder, leaned in and kissed her on the neck. She smiled in the way she used to do in the beginning of our relationship and that's when I knew. I knew who "R" in her mobile was. I recognized the asshole! Something just burst inside of me, Jack. I wanted to kill that son of a bitch."

"What do you mean, you just slept with her?"

"I know I'm weak, but when you called me, Jo was at my place. She wants me back she says."

"You slept with Jo? After she treated you like that?"

"Yeah, I know it's stupid." Mike looks down at his feet.

"I can't get my head around this shit. So you slept with Jo because she wants you back and then it turns out she's sleeping with Russell? What's wrong with this world?"

"Lots of things. I really thought she wanted me back, but when I saw him, I knew it was all just a lie."

Suddenly it dawned on my why Russell had been so secret with his texting and why he hadn't told me about his date - he was seeing my best friend's girlfriend. What a jerk!

"Mike, you have to promise me this: never ever see Joanne again. Promise me. You deserve so much better."

"I promise, I promise. Believe me, this was a true eye-opener."

"And here I was thinking you had had your wake-up call and you fell for her again. Crazy."

"Not everyone is as lucky as you are with women, Jack. Remember that."

That made me think of Cristina and feel sick with longing.

"You're right, Mike. I'm one lucky son-of-a-bitch."

***

Just getting out of the bed in the morning is a marathon and not even the usual double espresso can wake me up properly. I stand in front of my bathroom mirror and realize I look like a bum. My eyes are red and baggy and my skin is pale and dry, I even have two pimples on my cheek and I never had pimples before. I shave them off and let the blood run down my face, while I stare at my sorry self in the mirror. Is this really the attractive and successful advertising mogul who made such a buzz in the business a few years ago? Is it the same person? Maybe there's a vague resemblance in there somewhere and I need to pin my hope on that. Will my possibly last day in the office help or just make it worse? I'm about to find out.

I take my usual morning walk among my fellow stressed New Yorkers with their weapons of choice in hand – coffee thermoses, smartphones and cigarettes. I'm anxious about seeing familiar faces, what will they think of me showing up there? Surely the gossip must have spread like forest fire – the inevitable chatter about my strange, long "vacation".

I say hi to the doorman and he responds with a slightly nervous smile and a lame "Good morning Mr. Reynolds,"

He knows it too.

At least the elevator's empty, a small victory, because it would be a bad start to stand face to face with a co-worker in the cramped space. I travel 34 floors and hear the familiar bing! Doors open and here it comes, the lavender-scented air-freshener, the giant reception desk and the soft carpet underneath my shoes. It should feel like coming home, but I'm an alien now and this is far from where I belong.

The new strawberry-blonde receptionist confirms this. I don't know what happened to Anne, if she found a new job or got the foot, but it doesn't help my anxiety to see someone new in here, it just reminds me of the brevity of business life. I try to walk briskly past her.

"Good morning Mr. Reynolds!" she says far too loudly and it makes my heart jump in my chest. I don't know how she recognizes my face, maybe she has seen it on the famous wall of employee photos? I nod to her, force a smile and keep on walking. I need to pass by the open plan and get to my office with minimal human interaction, because I can't take any office small talk today. I'm already sweating, despite the air condition being on North Pole. It's like I'm suffocating in this suit, a 1500-dollar Hugo Boss which normally feels like second skin to me.

There's Tommy, waving at me from over at the copy machine with that stupid trademark smile on his face. I never liked him. Julie, one of the copywriters, gives me a brief look from behind her giant silver Apple screen. She has cut her red hair short, which looks a bit strange on her tiny head. Oh no, here comes Jim, posting a huge grin, looking like a big bad wolf ready to eat me.

"Hi man! So good to have you back!" He shakes my hand with the double grip and looks me in the eye. He's brimming with confidence. It's almost as if he was my superior and not vice versa and he has probably proven himself even more worthy of my position in my absence and stroked Nicholas ego both backwards and forwards. Is it maybe already set up? Is Jim planting my Judas kiss? Has Nicholas already made a deal with him? I wouldn't be surprised. Things happen so fast in this business, there's no time to be human and have breakdowns.

After shaking Jim's backstabbing hand I take a left turn and enter the last bit of corridor before my office.

At least here's Angela, my assistant, who I need more than ever on a day like this.

"Hi Angie, how are you?"

"Hi Jack," she says, "how was the vacation?" I like Angie, she's probably the only person I'm sad to leave behind.

"It was well needed," I say, flashing a smile.

"I've put a report for on your desk so you can read it when you get the time. It's probably good if you do it before your lunch with Nicholas. At least that's what he told me. Should I order up some coffee?" Angela is all business. And coffee.

"Yes, please."

My office is, as always, impeccably clean and fresh. I sit down in my expensive chair and think this might actually be the last time I do that. I let it mold itself around my body and I'm trying to feel *aaaaahhhh*, but I only feel *uuuughhh*. My desk is almost empty. Only the laptop and the report from Angela are taking up a small part of the massive space. Most of my colleagues have several pictures of family on their desks and I don't have one single item that would make my desk mine. This again reminds me how replaceable I am. And it makes me sad.

I look down on my laptop. I raise the lid and press the on-button and think here goes nothing.

Angela soon knocks on my door. I tell her to come in and after she puts the cup of coffee on my desk and turns to leave I say: "Angie?"

"Yes, boss?"

"Am I a good manager? I mean, was I ever nice to work with?"

"Of course. I like working with you very much, always have."

"Thanks. You know what? Take a half day today."

"Wow, that's nice of you. You don't have to do this - I like you anyway." Angela lets out a nervous laugh.

"Don't worry about it. Just promise me not to do any laundry, cleaning, or work-related stuff. I want you to enjoy it and relax. Why not spend it with friends or family?"

"Sure will. Thanks boss!"

Then she leaves me alone with the report.

***

The well-written document in front of me is a brain-hemorrhaging piece of depressing figures. I shouldn't care, I don't want to, but of course I do. The agency is partly my baby and I hate seeing it turning into a juvenile delinquent. Obese soft-drink marketing manager Brian ended up showing us the finger and hi-tech music player company tore up the contract, which means two big clients gone and none on the way. We're more or less screwed. Measures need to be taken, people's heads will have to roll. The lunch with Nicholas today should have been a crisis meeting if I felt I had an ounce of energy left to turn this ship around. But I don't and I'm desperate to be back with Cristina, so the only action I'll take is to resign from my position immediately. They shouldn't have a problem handing over to Jim, he for sure has the ambition and drive to succeed even in these dire circumstances.

I read another fifty e-mails and find nothing to change my mood or mind. There are so many things that need to be done, meetings which need to be held and actions that need to be taken. I'm feeling the tingles in my arm again and the breathing issue is back. I'm about to have a panic attack and I need to get out of here now.

I walk briskly out the door, through the corridor and past the open office space. I imagine my co-workers raising their heads and eyebrows and probably think, there goes the burnt-out nutcase again. I can't stand the wait for the elevator, so I run down the emergency stairs and out on the street. I'm dizzy, I'm sweating and I'm shaking. I walk in circles like a man needing to pee, then sit down on one of the benches outside and put my face in my hands and cry.

I sit there for a while, my face resting in my hands, my tears slowly drying. I'm a broken man on display and there's nothing to save my pride now. It's been mangled to pieces by recent events and the only way to get back from this is to move to Mexico, marry Cristina and start a new life.

Not that that's a bad thing, I just wanted my retirement to be a little more dignified.

When I manage to get myself together, I take a short walk around the area just to compose myself enough to head inside the office again. It's hard to describe the shame I feel as I pack the few personal items I have in my laptop bag and leave.

For the last time.

***

I'm meeting Nicholas at his favorite lunch place a few blocks away from the office. On my way there I'm writing a text to Cristina, telling her I'm about to resign and that I miss her so much I could cry (I don't tell her I already cried), when I bump straight into Stephen with his baby buggy. I don't recognize him at first. He has cut his hair real short and looks younger compared to the last time I saw him. His happy face hints to me that he must have solved those baby blues. I want to be happy for him, but I'm in a strange mood and I don't have much energy to spare.

He greets me with a wide smile.

"How's the baby?" I say, politely, and look inside the push-chair. It's funny, but I haven't even seen the infamous boy before. I'm not really into kids and have very little experience with babies, but I can safely say that Jeffrey is the ugliest baby I've ever come across. He was just unfortunate to get a mix of Stephen's Mickey Mouse ears and Maria's wide nose, which makes him look a bit like a cartoon character.

"Jeffrey is great and so am I," Stephen says, chipper as a chipmunk. "We're becoming very fond of each other in fact." Stephen looks lovingly down on his baby and seems so goddamn happy I want to jealousy-punch him in the face. I'm not jealous about having an ugly baby though, I'm jealous about someone being so worry-free.

I look at my watch and say: "Sorry Stephen, but I have to go, I have a lunch meeting."

"Ahaa," Stephen sounds disappointed. "Well, we ought to grab a beer sometime soon."

"Yes, sure," I say, "I'll call you," although I know it won't be soon, because I have too many other things on my mind, moving to Mexico being one of them.

So I leave Stephen and his ugly baby on the sidewalk and head across the street, pass by the glass Apple building and walk rapidly towards the restaurant when my phone vibrates in my pants pocket. I pick it up and find a text message from Cristina saying: "I can't wait to see you *mi amor*. I think about you all the time and my family is asking about you too. Hurry up! :) xxxxxx."

This sends a few butterflies down my nervous stomach. I can deal with anything right now, even a possibly disappointed business partner.

***

How do you tell your right hand man for many years that you're quitting on him? It's not easy, but I'm sure if there's someone who can handle the news well, it's Nicholas. He's tough, self-centered and has enough going on in his own life not to be too sentimental.

Nicholas' handshake is firm and confident. He's always dressed for success and the pinstriped suit he wears today is tailored to perfection. I've never seen Nicholas uncomfortable and when I see how alive and almost glowing he looks, I feel a bit jealous. Why not me? Why can't I be more in control?

Nicholas is always in control though. He puts care into every part of his appearance. He goes to the most expensive hairdressers to keep his wavy gold-brown hair look amazing, he uses expensive skin products and works out every day. I guess he's so at home with celebrities and royalty, because everything he does exudes class. Nicholas is a fierce careerist who can be ruthless if you bother him, but also a really nice guy if you happen to win his respect. I hope he still has an ounce of respect left for me.

When all the polite greetings are out of the way, I decide to flat out tell him I'm quitting the company. I don't know which reaction to expect, but Nicholas surprises me when he looks me straight in the eyes and says without a hint of emotion in his voice:

"I kind of knew this would happen, Jack. You've always poured your everything into this business and you are a big part in making it what it is today, but I have noticed how your efforts have slowly dwindled and so has the success of the company."

"When you just left the planet, I actually thought you might be gone forever. Not dead maybe, but finished. Angela told me you haven't been feeling well and since you weren't picking up the phone, I had to make other plans."

He gives me a look of pity - like he also wished I was more like him.

I don't know what to say, because I can't help but feel that I've let him down.

"So what's the plan?"

"I know you think Jim should take over the operations, but I have a friend of mine, Timothy Freed, who has plenty of experience with sinking ships and also some agency years behind him, and I think he has what it takes to turn it around. Some people will have to go of course and we'll need to restructure a bit, but with Tim at the wheel there's still hope." Nicholas recites this with less emotion than a robot. He couldn't care less that our good years together have passed. He is, first and foremost, a businessman.

"I have prepared some paperwork for you to sign. I'm basically buying you out and I'm giving you a fair deal here, since I could actually sue you for negligence." He puts a load of papers before me. "Just sign here and here, and we're done." He points out the lines I need to sign.

I'm suddenly sick to my stomach. I can't believe Nicholas is threatening me that if I don't sign the piece of paper, he will sue me! I thought we were friends on some level at least! But I have no energy to fight him either, because it's not about the money, it's about the way it's done. I read through the papers while he sips his wine and then I put my signature on the dotted line.

When I'm done, Nicholas stretches out his hand and says:

"Thank you for all these years, Jack. It's been quite a journey and I wish you the best of luck in the future."

I shake it, while I think that this wasn't how it was supposed to end.

Or was it?

***

That night I don't dream about Cristina, but of Gwen and when I wake up I know I need to see her. Not that I have any romantic feelings for her, but an important part of Jack 2.0 is to start with a clean slate and for that to happen I need to thank her for everything she did for me and apologize for how I treated her. I'm disappointed in myself for completely forgetting about her in the first place, but I guess there's been enough on my mind lately.

I decide a good start to cleaning my conscience would be telling Gwen how thankful I am for her help during that horrible night and how sorry I am I couldn't give her the kind of treatment she deserves.

So I text Gwen and ask her out for lunch. I suggest a typical business lunch place near Roosevelt center -

something to emphasize that this isn't a romantic lunch, just two friends catching up.

I'm not used to apologize, not in a sincere, "I was an asshole"-kind of way, so to cool my nerves I arrive early, order a GT and take a seat. I want to go through the conversation in my head before.

New York is bathing in sun today and I'm thirsty enough to manage a second drink before Gwen shows up, looking all business, both in dress and mood. She doesn't seem very impressed with me anymore and of course she has no reason to be. She's done something to her hair, cut it and dyed it darker. It looks okay on her, although I prefer the old, blonde look. She sits down and I tell her she looks great. She asks me how I'm feeling. I'm OK, I tell her.

Then I say this:

"Gwen, I want to start by saying both sorry and thank you. Thanks for being there for me when I was at my worst and sorry for not treating you with the respect you deserve. I was in a really bad spot there for a while, as you probably realized."

We're interrupted by Gwen's glass of Pepsi arriving.

"Was that what you wanted to say? Or are you looking for a third date?"

Gwen's blunt and sarcastic approach stops me in my tracks, but she continues before I get the chance to say anything.

"Don't bother replying, I knew from the first date what you think of me, you were so obviously bored from the second I opened my mouth. I know I can be quite a talker, especially when I'm nervous, but you didn't have to be so rude about it! It was the most immature date I've ever had! But don't worry about it,

I understand you're going through something right now."

We haven't even ordered the food before Gwen calls me both immature and rude. I guess I had to be ready for this, but I'm not.

"Why did you sleep with me then?"

"I was horny, Jack, and you're an attractive man. And to be honest with you, and this is the only compliment you deserve, you're quite good in bed. That's the only reason I called you out a second time. I guess I was also a bit curious, because I had never met a person like you before. But right from when we sat down I just felt sorry for you. I understood you were just a misunderstood boy in a rich man's costume. Then you had your weird attack and the rest is history."

A misunderstood boy in a suit? Surely she's just making shit up to protect her own feelings!

"I don't want to beat you up over it, but you obviously have some growing up to do before you start thinking about serious relationships and that's quite late for a guy close to his 40s." Gwen gives me a nonchalant look - she's butchering me and she's enjoying it.

"35. I'm 35." Is what I manage to say as a lame reprieve to the onslaught. I can't believe I thought she was crazy about me and I hurt her, when it couldn't have been further from the truth.

The waiter comes back and asks for our order, but Gwen says she only has time for the Pepsi. We're both dying to get out of here.

The blood is boiling in my veins and I really want to throw some nasty insults back at Gwen, but somehow I think of Jack 2.0 and Cristina and I manage to restrain myself.

"I'm sorry I'm such a dick," I say, slightly sarcastically, "and that's why I asked you to come here, nothing else."

"Apology accepted," Gwen says, less angry now. She got it all out of her system.

"So now that we got that out of the way, you're free to go. I'll pay for the Pepsi." I tell her, thankful we didn't order a proper lunch.

Gwen finishes her soft drink, says goodbye and leaves me alone to think about what a deranged person I am.

Luckily, I'm upgrading.

***

The next few days passes quickly. I'm sorting out paperwork, packing bags, talking a bit to my father and a lot to Cristina. My phone bill will be astronomical, but it's probably the best spent money of my life. I book tickets to Mexico and prepare myself emotionally to live in another country. I even buy a Spanish language course to struggle with during the day.

Two days before I'm about to leave, I book a night out with Mike at a nice rooftop restaurant. We need a proper goodbye, because he's what I'm most sad to leave right now.

Mike looks happy and relaxed as we meet outside the posh lounge restaurant and judging by his physical appearance, there's no doubt he's been exercising. Maybe he really did buy an exercise bike?

"You look great." I say.

"Thanks! This gym membership is slowly making wonders. And you should see the girls there!" Mike smiles. He hasn't only shed physical weight, but also emotional.

"Hehe, you know there's only one girl for me nowadays." I say as we're shown to our table. I think of Cristina and smile.

"Tonight is a night for celebration. It's your going-away-party, I'm feeling pretty elated for some reason and therefore we shall drink like kings!" Mike says and scans the wine list.

"We shall!" I say, feeling happy and excited.

We order a bottle of very expensive French wine and a rib-eye each.

"Everything ready for the trip? You have the apartment keys?" Mike asks me.

"Yes, everything should be fine and dandy. And I brought the keys with me actually." Mike is going to be my apartment caretaker while I'm gone, so I've duplicated my keys.

"Crazy this."

"Yes, I feel it's the only thing I can do, but it's been a couple of hellish days. Just leaving my job turned me into a wreck and when I met Gwen the other day, she gave me an earful about what a lousy bastard I am."

"You met with Gwen?" Mike stares at me with incredulous eyes.

"Yeah, I wanted to apologize. I feel I need a clean slate."

"Wow, that's impressive. But if you're going to apologize to everyone you've hurt over the years, you have quite a task in front of you!" Mike chuckles. But I know he's half-serious.

"Ha-ha, very funny. I have to draw the line somewhere and I'm starting with Gwen."

"Good for you and good for her!" Mike says and raises his glass.

We clink our glasses and look out over the city. At the same time the food arrives.

"You really think you're going to be able to leave this place?" Mike says, digging into this meat.

"I think I have to. I can always come back, but I need to open my mind a bit, that's been the main problem for me over the years, I've been stuck with picturing exactly the life I would lead here. And when I had the life I wanted, I realized it wasn't enough."

I feel my phone vibrate in my pocket. I pick it up and the display reads: "Melody".

"I need to take this," I say to Mike and point to my phone, "It's Melody," I whisper.

"Oh." Mike whispers back.

I step away from our table to a quieter place along the edge of the terrace and take the call.

"Hi Melody, how are you?" I say casually.

"Jack," she says, sounding like she's in panic mode, "Are you alone, are you sitting down?" Oh shit! Has something happened to dad? Oh shit, oh shit, oh shit.

"Yes, I'm alone," I say anxiously. I look around and see there are at least a few meters between me and other people, "but I'm standing. What's going on?"

"I'm pregnant, Jack."

My mind is sucked into a tunnel.

"Jack? Jack? Are you there?"

"You're pregnant?" My voice is remarkably calm for someone deciding whether he's going to jump over the railing or not.

"Yes, I am. It's yours."

I try to form words, but no words can describe what I feel, which is like traveling outside my body, watching myself standing there, talking on the phone, looking like a fool.

"Before you say anything," Melody says brusquely, "I want to keep the child." Her voice has quickly gone from panic to determination, while my tongue is stuck to the back of my mouth. "I can raise the child with Hank if you don't want to be there for it, but I really want this baby."

Melody's aggression is what wakes me up. "Are you crazy? Are you going to raise my baby with my father?"

"I'm definitely not crazy, but you are who doesn't want this baby!"

"I haven't said that, I'm just saying it's crazy! This situation is fucked up! We need to think this through properly before we jump to conclusions." I look around to see if anyone's listening.

"Yeah, just you go to your Mexican slut! Don't you worry about the baby, you do what's best for you, exactly like you always do." Melody is panicking again. In a furious way.

"Mel, listen to me, Mel! We'll solve this! If this is my baby and you're not bullshitting me, we'll find a way. But I need to think about it and I want you to think about it too. Don't go nuts now, okay? Don't tell Hank or anything. In fact don't do anything. We can talk tomorrow, OK? I will call you first thing. Promise." Now I'm panicking and it's pretty obvious.

"Call me first thing then, okay? Otherwise I'll tell Hank. We're supposed to go out to dinner tomorrow evening and it's going to be weird if I suddenly don't drink wine. He's going to think it's his."

"Okay, okay. I'll call you."

And we say goodbye.

Mike is eager for information when I get back to the table. "What was that all about? You look like you've seen a naked fat person." I sit down with unsteady legs and grab my wine glass and empty it.

"I'm going to be a father." I say, in a dead tone. I'm feeling completely empty inside.

"Come again?"

"Melody is pregnant and she says the baby is mine. I'm going to be a father."

Now it's Mike's turn to finish his glass of wine in one swift motion.

"Are you serious? This can't possibly be happening. Why doesn't she just have an abortion?"

"Because she doesn't want to! Because she's gone fucking crazy!"

"But that's fucked up! She can't just have your kid like that. You must have some say!" We're both pretty drunk, but the call from Melody is sobering us up fast.

"She just asked me to be there, to take responsibility for it. I don't know if she wants us to be together or what. I don't know anything except for that she's completely nuts. And pregnant."

"You know what?" I say to Mike and push my plate of half-eaten rib-eye away, "Can we pick up the bill and go for a walk or something? I'm feeling a bit sick."

"Sure, but you might want to finish the bottle?" He pours me another glass and I empty it - feeling nothing.

***

Mike and I are walking down Fifth Avenue. I'm freaking out. I'm shivering and my chest is tightening again. I'm worried I'm about to have another attack, this time fatal.

Suddenly, I feel a punch to my stomach and I throw up right there on the sidewalk among a few puzzled and disgusted New Yorkers. Mike puts his hands under my armpits and pulls me up from the ground. I wipe remnants of smelly yellow vomit from my mouth, while he helps me away from the small scene I've created. He doesn't say anything, which I welcome at this moment. What do you say to a person who's falling apart right before your eyes? There's no comfort in words, that's for sure.

We hail a cab and go back to my penthouse. The place is impeccably clean and there are two suitcases on the floor. Suitcases I was about to bring with me to Mexico. But how can I go to Mexico now? What can I tell Cristina? What will my father say? It slowly dawns on me that Melody can't have this baby, because it will ruin absolutely everything I hoped my life would become.

Everything.

***

I wake up hoping I'm somewhere else, that everything that happened yesterday was just a dream, another nightmare. But soon I know everything did indeed happen, because I find Mike sleeping on the couch with his mouth open, snoring like a drunken sailor.

I'm going to be a father. I'm going to be a father. I'm going to be father.

The thought strikes me like a hammer to the chest and leaves me breathless.

While I wait for the thick black java to spill out of my Nespresso machine, I look out the kitchen window on this crisp and sunny October morning. On a normal day, I would have felt like taking a walk through the park, but all I can do today is sit down at my kitchen table with my espresso and my morning paper and stare into thin air. I glance down at the paper, almost expecting the headline to read: Another Meteor Strikes On Jack Reynolds. But it doesn't, the strike is really about underpaid teachers and I can't help but think that these teachers don't know how good they have it - if only my problem was money.

After drinking my coffee and doing some more staring, I see Mike's showing signs of life by scratching his hairy ass.

"Morning," I say without emotion.

"Morning," he says, also in a somber tone. Then he tries to climb out of the sofa and ends up falling on the floor with a thump. He moans and I can't help but laugh.

"You see, you still have some laughter in you," he says.

"That was probably the last bit. Reserved for you falling on your fat ass."

"I aim to please," Mike says. "How are you feeling by the way?" he adds, giving me a concerned look you would give someone with a deadly disease.

"Not great. I have to call Melody and try to bribe the child away. It's the only solution as I see it."

"Yeah, that could work. If talking to her doesn't. And you obviously need to do a paternity test."

"I wish I could put faith in a test like that, but I somehow feel the baby must be mine. And sadly, my hope for talking sense to her after our psycho conversation yesterday is almost gone. But I'll give it everything I've got, of course. You want coffee?"

"Damn right I do."

***

My hands are trembling as I'm typing a text message to Melody. It's not a poetic masterpiece, it's just, "can I call you?", but I'm still nervous, picturing the upcoming conversation in my head, thinking of how to phrase what could be the most important sales call of my life. I shoot the text out into cyberspace and receive a reply within a minute: "In 10."

I'm pacing back and forth in my penthouse, a thing I do when I'm nervous. Mike has gone to pick up breakfast and I'm alone in the apartment. Alone with my thoughts and this dreaded phone call.

When twelve minutes have passed at the speed of a snail on a sandpaper track racing against the wind, I place the call. Melody picks up on the first ring, eager to hear what I have to say.

"Mel, I've been thinking, I've been thinking hard. There's simply no way we can have this baby. I can't break my father's heart and I don't think you want that either. But I understand I've put you in a very difficult situation and I'm of course more than willing to help you out of it. Just tell me the amount you want and I'll sort out all the hospital costs, everything."

Melody's reply is not what I hoped for: "You're trying to buy away your child? Is that how your sick mind works, Jack?"

The bribe apparently failed miserably. I should have tried to small talk to her first, eased her into it - but I was too nervous.

Time to backpedal.

"No, don't get me wrong. I'm just saying there's no way we can do this. I can't do this to my father and it's not fair to the baby."

"Fair to the baby? You don't even want the baby, so what do you care? I'm not going to kill a baby just because you won't accept the responsibility. I'll raise it with Hank and you can go live in Mexico or whatever you want to do with your sorry life."

Suddenly I realize Melody could be pro-life, which means I'm completely and utterly fucked.

Fucked. Fucked. Fucked.

"But you can't threaten me like this! It's my baby too for God's sake! And it's not even a baby yet, not until a certain time has passed - don't you realize that? Do you really see raising this child with my father as an option? Don't you understand how sick that sounds?"

I'm really panicking now. I'm starting to think there's no way out of it. And Melody is not budging.

"Jack, I believe in life. This baby is a blessing and I'm not going kill it. It's up to you whether or not you want to share it with me. That's what I can offer you."

"Seriously Mel, what the fuck! What is it you really want? You want us to be together? Is that it?"

Melody starts crying.

"Of course I want you, Jack. I want to raise this child with you. It's our baby! But I'm being nice to you, giving you the chance to escape and live your life."

Oh, shit. It's over. My life is over.

"Listen to me, Mel. I need to think about this and I need to see you in person for us to properly discuss it. Can you figure something out? Can you come to New York? Take the first flight out, leave a note for my father. Tell him you had to go see your family or something."

Melody's voice is instantly softer, "I'll try. I need to see you too."

"We'll work this thing out, okay?"

"Okay."

And when we hang up, Melody has stopped crying, but I'm close to.

***

I call Cristina and tell her I have to postpone my flight. I say there's some paperwork I have to sort out, but that I'll reschedule my trip as near in the future as possible. She cries on the other end, which almost makes me weep too, but there's nothing else I can do - I first need to solve the mess I've created for myself.

Melody texts me and writes that she's managed to book a flight for tomorrow, early morning.

I don't know what I'm going to do. I try to look at my problem from every possible angle, but it's like a maze without an exit - no matter what I do, I'm stuck.

I lose.

I lose Cristina.

I lose my father.

I lose everything I believe in.

All because of one stupid mistake.

***

I wake up, sweating puddles, from another vivid dream of Cristina, of Mexico, of a baby I never asked for, of betraying my father – everything melting together in weird sequences and shapes. My heart's thumping and my mind's aching, but this is purely psychological pain, nothing else and I don't think there's much of a cure.

Mike knows there's nothing he can do, still he calls to check on me every now and then. No matter how helpful he can be, this is my shit to clean up. All the bad karma I've spread through my life has come right back at me, like a boomerang of evil gathering momentum.

I walk through Central Park and it looks different to me. Darker. The shadows more menacing than before.

I sit down on a bench and tell myself what I have to do. I'll tell the truth. I'll come clean. And I'll pay the price.

***

I only call for my sister when I feel really lonely, sorry for myself or when I need something, and she knows this, but maybe she senses something is extra wrong this time, because she agrees to see me on very short notice.

I meet her at one of the Starbucks in Greenwich Village, not far from where she lives with her band-playing boyfriend. For the record, my sister doesn't look anything like me. She has reddish, almost orange hair, green eyes and freckles – all from the thin strands of Irish genes running through the Reynolds family. I think she got almost all the Irish blood.

Karen is already at a small, checkered table with her sketchpad when I get there. I'm 15 minutes late and apologize with a hug. It feels nice to hold my sister and I guess I'm in a state where I need to cling onto all the love I can get. In fact I should collect it and bottle it for emergency situations.

I order a double espresso and a still water and head back to Karen and her sketchpad.

"What are you drawing?"

"It's kind of a cool project. We're doing concept art for a movie and right now I'm trying to get this armor to look right using a technique called cross-hatching."

"It looks good," I say absentmindedly. "I heard dad called you." It feels weird not to have talked to my sister about this before, I should've called her myself just after it happened and she's right to be pissed that I didn't.

"Yes, I talked to him. He's feeling better. I would've appreciated if either of you had called me sooner."

"I know, I'm sorry. I had a little bit too much on my hands to be honest with you."

"You always have too much, Jack."

"Believe me, this time I really did."

And so I tell her everything. Every little shitty detail I can remember. I tell her how I broke down during my blind date with Gwen, how I slept with my father's girlfriend, the one he intends to marry, how I fell in love with Cristina and ended up planning my move to Mexico. I tell her how I quit my job and how Melody called me out of the blue, announcing her pregnancy and her unwillingness to "kill our baby". I scoop out my soul and put it right there on the table for my sister to see and for perhaps the first time in our lives, I feel us connecting on a deeper level. There are tears in her eyes when I'm finished and there are tears in mine too. We're both drained of energy and emotion and Karen actually reaches over and holds my hand. It's a small gesture, but it means the world to me.

If only it could change it all.

***

The next day Melody texts me and writes that she'll be late. She will be taking a later flight and will arrive in the evening. I'm anxious to meet her and talk to her, but there's nothing I can do about it. Cristina calls me again, asking about my paperwork, and it's with great strain I tell her there are still some details to sort out, but that I should have a date by tomorrow. I can hear in her voice that she doesn't quite believe me - a part of her probably afraid I'll bail out and break up with her instead.

I'm not going to break up with her, because I love her, but I have to tell her the truth. There's no way around that. And when I do, there's a huge risk she'll break up with me.

And then I'll die inside.

***

I'm sitting in my sofa, drinking a glass of red, trying to relax, when there's a knock on the door. It's with heavy steps I walk over and open it.

It's Melody. She puts down her luggage on the floor and throws her arms around me. I cannot really mimic the gesture, but give her a polite hug.

She removes her clothes and sits down in the sofa.

"Wine?" I ask her.

"I can't." she says and smiles nervously.

"Yeah, shit. I forgot."

I pour her a glass of water instead and sit down opposite her.

"He knows." Melody says.

"What?"

"Your father knows. He knows about us and the baby." She's remarkably calm when she says this.

"You told him?" I almost shout. Anger pulsates through me and I feel like throwing her against the wall.

"I had to. There was no other way. He cried and I cried and then he threw me out on my ass. He hasn't tried to call you?"

You stupid bitch! I feel like screaming, but the anger quickly turns to sadness. Sadness for my father. For everything.

"No, he hasn't. I'd imagine he doesn't want anything to do with me ever again."

"He'll forgive you. I know he will. He has too much love and understanding for you."

"But how could you tell him without asking me first? That was the point of you coming here!"

"I'm sorry, but he started asking questions about why I didn't drink. And he looked so happy for a while, because he somehow knew I was pregnant and he assumed it was his child, and I couldn't stand seeing that look on his face any longer. I just *had* to tell him."

"And you're absolutely sure it's my child and not his?"

"Of course! A hundred percent. It's the only way it adds up with the days. We don't have sex that often you know, me and your father."

I push the mental images away. "Thanks, but I'd rather not hear about that and I can promise you I'll do a paternity test."

"I understand."

I look at her and she looks at me and at that moment she knows I don't love her, at least not the way she wants me to, and she starts crying.

And I go over to her and hold her for a long time with a sinking feeling in my stomach that I'm not sure can ever go away.

***

The phone call to Cristina is the worst thing I've done in my life. She can't believe what I'm telling her, that the Jack she knows is so stupid and so morally corrupt that he sleeps with his father's girlfriend. I can't blame her for not believing me either, it's so insane the whole situation that I can't really expect anyone to, least of all the love of my life.

I tell her I don't have any true romantic feelings for Melody, that we'll just "organize" the parenting situation, but Cristina of course sees through it all: "Do you honestly think I'm that stupid? You're going to have a child with this woman, Jack, you're going to raise a baby together. And you're definitely not going to do that from Mexico. I can't believe you even say these things. What kind of person are you? You fooled me all along. Well done!"

She cry and I cry. She shout at me that I'm the lowest lowlife at the bottom of the sea. She tells me she hates me. I'm a liar, a devil, an idiot, a fool and many other bad things. She says I should be glad I'm not near her, because she would kill me. And that she can't believe she brought me into her home.

I want to kill myself. Cristina is the only woman who's made me feel truly in love and now I've ruined everything by not keeping my troublemaker in my pants. I've alienated and hurt two of the people I love the most and now I'm going to bring a child into this world and into very unclear parental circumstances. I have really gone and done it all.

Cristina tells me she never wants to hear from me again and hangs up. I sit down on the floor and put my head in my hands and cry. Because what else can I do?

And when Melody comes home from her shopping later that evening, I leave without saying a word to her.

Instead I go to a bar and drink my head into oblivion.

***

Months pass. Melody and I live together in my apartment and we fight a lot. We fight about everything, about kids' names, about how we're going to sort out accommodation after the child is born, how we're going to divide our time.

They're all practical things, devoid of emotion.

The paternity test tells me I'm going to be a father for sure, but somehow I never doubted it.

In a desperate attempt to clear out my sick mind, I start writing a diary, summarizing the events leading up to this "unwanted" baby and the uncertain future it's about to enter. I call my father, but he refuses to answer. My sister says he's still angry and that I need to give him more time.

I make one of the bedrooms in the penthouse into a baby room. We argue about the color. We know it's going to be a girl, but Melody doesn't want the room to be pink. I think it should be pink, it needs to be pink, if just for argument's sake.

In reality I know a lot of our fights are built from my resentment, the way Melody insisted on having this baby, and thereby ruining my relationship both with my dad and Cristina. A little part of me hates her for it, although she's going to be the mother of my child.

I'm also angry at myself of course. Furious. My lousy self-control ruined my life, destroyed my chance at happiness, and because of that I'm permanently in a shitty mood.

Mike tells me I need to get over it, that I need to find peace with myself and the situation, but although I know he's right, I refuse to. I won't let God, or whoever's in charge, have his way. It's my life, my fate, and I want to control it.

But I can't. And I can't control Melody's pregnant mood swings either. Sometimes I feel like punching her or forcing her to kill the baby, so this farce can stop. So we can go separate ways and just live our lives.

But we can't. We're stuck together for better or worse.

More months pass.

And the baby is born.

***

But not everything is gloomy in the end.

Yes, isn't it the damndest thing how life works? A little baby arrives and things change. The world becomes more colorful. Food tastes better. Songs sound sweeter.

Suddenly I see life through Amber's blue eyes. Everything is new, different and exciting. You could say we were born together, Amber and I. I'm now Jack 3.0, the father and it's first role in my life I really warm to.

I wish I could say the same for my relationship with Melody, that the ending of this book could be sweeter, more Hollywood. But there has been too much water under the bridge, too many strange mistakes, too much pain. So although we live together and love our baby and try to make things work – I don't think it's going to.

But then again, what this period in my life has taught me is that I simply cannot know what cards I will be dealt next. All I can try to do is to manage them better.

I've tried to reach out to my father and although he has talked to me and we've cleared the air a little – our relationship is tainted. Maybe he will never completely forgive me, maybe it will take a few years. I know I will try my best – because I need him in my life and Amber needs him in her life too.

What I've learned from all this is that I need to work hard on my relationships and not only on my career. I need to live my life differently.

I *want* to tell you that I've forgotten about Cristina, that all my focus is on patching things up with my father and being the best father in the world to Amber. I want to tell you that and mean it. But I can't, because Cristina is very much still on my mind from time to time. I keep kicking myself for how I ruined things with her, but then I look at Amber and see the best thing that ever happened to me and stop.

It's confusing. It's painful. It's maybe karma's way of getting back at me.

Talking about Cristina, I received an e-mail from her the other day. She had seen my recently published management book in the stores and wrote that she's thinking of me from time to time and what could've been. It evidently still makes her sad, the way it ended between us. Not that she hasn't moved on in the practical sense - she's apparently dating a local political hotshot (a friend of her father), but she tells me it's not the same. She ends her e-mail by saying she hopes I'm well and that I haven't forgotten about her.

I don't think I ever will.

But I don't want to end this book with something so gloomy as my uncertainty about the future. There are many bright spots in my life too. My love for Amber, my improved connection with my sister and my friendship with Mike is getting stronger by the day. These are things I'm endlessly grateful for.

As this story tells you, I haven't always been grateful in the past so that's a big step for me - a major lesson learned for the events described here.

And I guess this shows that there's hope for all of us, that we can all wake up and aspire to be better people and live more fulfilling lives, no matter how tough and complicated they may be.

All we need to do, is answer our wake-up calls.

THE END.

ABOUT THE AUTHOR

Jonas is currently the creative director of one of the most successful online gaming groups in the world. He has previously worked as a copywriter and a journalist. When he's not working he cherishes every moment with his family Lenah and Aiden and whatever time there's left he spends writing, reading and playing tennis. He's passionate about traveling and wine and thinks New York is the greatest city in the world. He lives with his family on the Mediterranean island of Malta. You can read more about Jonas through his blog at **jonaswrites.com**